His hand reached out and ever so gently cupped my cheek.

A shiver of reaction coursed through me, but for some reason I still didn't move away. It was like I was under his spell. Totally under his control, with no will to snap out of it. The pad of his thumb moved over the circle of my chin, not quite touching my lower lip but close enough for it to go into raptures of tingling, fizzing anticipation. His eyes remained focussed on my mouth, as if he too were recalling how it felt against his.

Was he going to kiss me? Would I allow him to? I was in a conundrum. I wanted to feel his mouth on mine if for no other reason than to prove to myself that I'd been imagining it had felt far more amazing than it actually had. I guess I also wanted to prove to myself that I could resist him. That I could withstand the commanding pressure of his mouth and not melt into a pool of mush.

But another shockingly traitorous part of me wanted to close the distance between our mouths and give myself up to the storm of passion I could feel building inside my body. It was surging through my blood, firing up all my senses, making me giddy with longing. A longing I could feel pounding deep in my core.

Dear Reader,

One of the things I love about being a writer is that I never have to look very far for the characters for my stories. They nearly always come looking for me. Jem Clark is one such character.

I wrote Jem's younger sister Bertie's story, *A Date with Her Valentine Doc*, with the intention of it being a one-off first person Mills & Boon® Medical Romance™ especially for St Valentine's Day. (By the way, I had *so* much fun writing that story!) But right from the start Jem was there, with her story just waiting to be told. In fact she was so real to me I sent an email to my editor using her voice!

Jem is a strong and sharp-tongued young woman with a take-no-prisoners attitude. You have been warned!

Thankfully, I didn't have to look very far for my hero Alessandro Lucioni. My Mills & Boon® Modern™ Romance readers will already know how much I love an Italian alpha hero—and a deeply tortured one even more so.

I hope you enjoy *Italian Surgeon to the Stars* as much as I enjoyed writing it.

Warmest wishes

Melanie Milburne

ITALIAN
SURGEON
TO THE STARS

BY
MELANIE MILBURNE

First published in Great Britain 2015
by Mills & Boon, an imprint of Harlequin (UK) Limited,
Eton House, 18-24 Paradise Road, Richmond, Surrey, TW9 1SR

© 2015 Melanie Milburne

ISBN: 978-0-263-25822-6

Harlequin (UK) Limited's policy is to use papers that are natural,
renewable and recyclable products and made from wood grown in
sustainable forests. The logging and manufacturing processes conform
to the legal environmental regulations of the country of origin.

From as soon as **Melanie Milburne** could pick up a pen she knew she wanted to write. It was when she picked up her first Mills & Boon® at seventeen that she realised she wanted to write romance. After being distracted for a few years by meeting and marrying her own handsome hero, surgeon husband Steve, and having two boys, plus completing a Masters of Education and becoming a nationally ranked athlete (Masters' swimming), she decided to write. Five submissions later she sold her first book and is now a multi-published, bestselling, award-winning *USA TODAY* author. In 2008 she won the Australian Readers' Association most popular category/series romance, and in 2011 she won the prestigious Romance Writers of Australia R*BY award.

Melanie loves to hear from her readers via her website, melaniemilburne.com.au, or on Facebook: facebook.com/melanie.milburne

Books by Melanie Milburne

Mills & Boon® Medical Romance™

A Date with Her Valentine Doc
Flirting with the Socialite Doc
Dr Chandler's Sleeping Beauty
Sydney Harbour Hospital: Lexi's Secret
The Surgeon She Never Forgot
The Man with the Locked Away Heart

Visit the author profile page at millsandboon.co.uk for more titles

To Amy Thompson—a fellow poodle-lover,
a fantastic friend and a fabulous beauty therapist. You
are one of the sweetest and kindest people I know. xxx

CHAPTER ONE

EVEN THOUGH I'M a fully qualified teacher I still hate getting called into the headmistress's office. I get this nervous prickle in my stomach, like a bunch of ants are tiptoeing around in there on stilettos. My knees feel woolly and unstable. My heart starts to hammer.

It's a programmed response from my childhood. I was rubbish at school. I mean *really* rubbish. Which is kind of ironic since I ended up a teacher at the prestigious Emily Sudgrove School for Girls in Bath, but that's another story.

Being called in to the office nearly always means there's a problem with one of the parents—a complaint or a criticism over how I'm handling one of their little darlings. Everyone knows helicopter parents are bad news. But, believe me, fighter pilot ones are even worse.

I stood outside the closed door and took a calming breath before I knocked on the door and entered.

'Ah, here she is now,' said Miss Fletcher, the headmistress, with a polished professional smile. 'Jem, this is Dr Alessandro Lucioni—a new parent.'

The words were like a closed-fist punch to my heart. *Bang.* I'm sure it missed a beat. Maybe two. Possibly three. I stood there with a blank expression on my face…or at least I hoped it was blank. God forbid I should show any sign of the shock that was currently rocketing through me.

Alessandro was a parent? A father? He was married? He was in love?

The words were like a ticker tape running through my head. But then it flipped off its spool and flickered in a tangled knot inside my head. One of the stray tapes wrapped itself around my heart and squeezed until it hurt.

Alessandro gave a formal nod and held out a hand. 'Miss Clark.'

I stared at his hand. That hand had known every inch of my body. That hand had coached me to my first orgasm. Those long, clever fingers had made me feel things I hadn't felt before or since. The sight of that hand made memories I'd locked away twist and writhe and wriggle out of their shackles and run amok with my emotions. I could feel the spread of heat flowing through me. Furnace-hot heat. Heat that made me acutely aware of my sexuality and the needs and urges I usually staunchly, stubbornly, *furiously* ignored.

I brought my gaze up to his unreadable one. So he wasn't going to let on that he knew me. Biblically or literally. Fine. I would play the same game.

'Welcome to Emily Sudgrove,' I said, and put my hand in his. His fingers were cool and strong, and closed around mine with just enough pressure to remind me of the sensual power he'd once had over me.

Okay. Forget about once. I admit it. He *still* had it over me. I felt the tingle of the contact. The nerves of my fingers and hand were lighting up like fairy lights on a tree. Sparking. Fizzing. Wanting.

'Thank you,' he said, with a brief flicker of his lips that passed for a smile—but I noticed it didn't make the distance to his eyes.

Oh, dear Lordy me, his eyes! They were a dark lustrous brown. Darker than chocolate. Strong eyes. Eyes that could melt frozen butter like a blowtorch. Eyes that could be sexily hooded and smouldering when he was in the mood for sex. Eyes that could make my blood sing through my veins with just a look.

I felt his gaze move over my face in an assessing manner. I hoped he wasn't noticing my eyebrows needed shaping. Why hadn't I made the time for a bit of lady landscaping? Why, oh, why hadn't I used the hair straightener that morning? My hair is my biggest bugbear. I *hate* my corkscrew curls. For most of my life I've had to endure dumb blonde jokes. At least when I tame my hair it gives me a little more credibility, or so I like to think.

Think. Now, there's an idea. But my brain wasn't capable of rational thought. I was in fight-or-flight mode. I wanted to get away from Alessandro—as I'd been doing for the last five years.

I'd seen glimpses of him from time to time. He'd saved the life of a London theatre actor a couple of years ago, which had made him into a celebrity doctor. He's a heart surgeon. A pretty darn good one too—I have to give him that. He ripped *my* heart right out of my chest without anaesthetic. Oh, and the reason he's called 'Dr', and not Mr like other surgeons, is because he's done a PhD on top of his arduous training.

Talk about an overachiever. And people think *I'm* a workaholic. I reckon his business card would have to be one of those fold-out concertina ones, like those old-fashioned postcards, to accommodate all the letters after his name.

I saw him just a couple of weeks ago in Knightsbridge, when I was having lunch with my younger sister Bertie. He didn't see me, thank God. He was with a blonde. A gorgeous supermodel type, with legs up to her armpits and perfect skin, perfectly shaped eyebrows and perfectly smooth straight hair. The type of woman he's been seen out and about with ever since our relationship. Luckily my sister didn't recognise him—or if she did she knew better than to say anything.

Urgh. I hate thinking about my relationship with Alessandro. I hate even using that term. It wasn't a relationship—not for him, anyway. I was a rebound. That's another word I loathe. I was a consolation prize. Not Miss Right, but Miss Will Do.

'Dr Lucioni has enrolled his niece into your class, Jem,' Miss Fletcher said into the canyon of silence.

Niece?

An inexplicable sense of relief collided with shock. He had a sister? A niece? Relatives? He'd told me he was an orphan.

I'd been amazed at how well he had done for himself when he had no one to back him. Not many people get to where he has without a leg-up somewhere along the way. But on the rare occasions when he spoke of his past he'd told me his parents died when he was a teenager and he had put himself through school and then medical school by working three jobs. There was no family money. No extended family support.

What other lies had he fed me?

I looked at him with a quizzical frown. 'You have a sister?'

Something moved at the back of his eyes, like a stagehand darting back into the shadows behind the curtains between acts.

'Yes,' he said. 'She's currently unwell, and I'm taking care of Claudia until she recovers.'

His voice... *Holy guacamole.* His voice was like a caress to my sex-starved body. It stroked over me like a sensual hand, making the base of my spine melt like a marshmallow in front of a campfire. The deepness of it, the mellifluous tone of it, the Sicilian accent even years living outside his homeland hadn't been able to remove.

That voice had told me things I had no business believing. I had fallen for every word. Every shallow promise I had taken to heart. I was ashamed of how stupid I'd been. Deeply and cringingly ashamed.

I'd spent years scoffing at my hippie parents for falling for the latest fad and then I'd gone and done the same. I'd latched on to Alessandro like a directionless follower does a guru. I'd worshipped him. I'd been prepared to give up all I had to be with him. I would have walked—no, crawled on my knees—over glass or razorblades or burning coals or a pit of hissing vipers to be with him.

But what I'd thought we had was a sham. It was all smoke and mirrors. He hadn't loved me at all. I was payback to the woman who'd dumped him for a richer man.

'Claudia will be boarding with us,' Miss Fletcher said.

I swung my gaze back to Alessandro's. 'Boarding?'

His expression gave nothing away. 'I work long, sometimes unpredictable, hours at the hospital.'

I teach six and seven-year-olds. Key Stage One as we call it in the UK. Grade One in the US and other parts of the world. I know children in the UK go to boarding school a lot younger than anywhere else, but sometimes it's a good thing. *Sometimes.* If a family is dysfunctional or not coping with the demands of kids then a well-run boarding school is a good option. Maybe even the best option in some cases. But I worry about kids who are shunted off before they're emotionally ready.

Boarding school can be a brutal place for a child who is overly sensitive. I have a history of oversensitivity, so I kind of know about these things.

Mind you, I never went to boarding school. Maybe if I had my childhood would have been a little less chaotic. My sister and I were hauled out of school when we were six and seven respectively and taken off to live in a commune in the Yorkshire moors, where we were supposed to learn through play. We were there two whole years before the authorities tracked us down and stepped in.

My sister Bertie's playing and learning was clearly of a much higher standard than mine, because she was a year ahead of her peers when she was placed back in the system. Unfortunately I was behind. Way, *way* behind. It took me years to catch up, and even now whenever I don't know the answer to something I get that same sinking sensation in the pit of my stomach—a feeling of inadequacy, of not being smart enough, of not quite making the grade.

It doesn't take a psychotherapist to understand why I chose to teach at a posh girls' school. I needed to prove to myself that I was good enough to teach in one of the best schools in the country. But the thing I've come to realise is that it doesn't matter how rich or poor your parents are—children are the same world over.

Some are strong academically; others, like me, can wangle the social side to their advantage. I made the art of fitting in into a science. I totally nailed it. Even though at times I compromised myself.

Alessandro was watching me with that same unfathomable expression on his face. Why had he chosen my school? There were dozens of boarding schools across the country. Why The Emily Sudgrove School for Girls in Bath? He worked in one of London's top hospitals. He lived in Belgravia. Yes, Belgravia. I told you he'd done well for himself. Why didn't he enrol his niece in a school closer to where he lived?

'Dr Lucioni would like a tour of the school,' Miss Fletcher said.

Her name was Clementine, but no one was allowed to call her that. She was proudly single and preferred Miss to Ms. She believed in formal address from her staff to establish respect, although she always called us by our Christian names when the children weren't around.

'Will you see to that, Jem?' she added.

'Sure,' I said brightly.

See how good I am at playing the game? Show no fear. That was my credo. It comes in pretty useful as a teacher too. You'd be surprised at how knee-knockingly scary some six or seven-year-olds can be. Although nothing compares to a six-foot-three hot Sicilian guy you once had monkey sex with, but still...

'Come this way,' I said.

I felt him just behind me as I walked out of the office. If I stopped he would cannon into me. I was tempted to stop. It had been a long time since a man had touched me, even by accident. I'm no nun, but neither have I been getting out there much. Not lately. Not since...

I had to really think before I could remember. Ah, yes, I remember now. I had a blind date with a friend of a friend's older brother a couple of years ago. God, what a disaster *that* was. No wonder I don't like remembering it. He was on something illegal and kept leaving the table where we were having dinner to have another snort. It took me a while to realise what was going on. The third time he said he needed the bathroom I ordered the most expensive wine on the wine list, drank half a glass and then left him to sort out the bill. I don't let men walk all over me any more. I get in first.

Speaking of illegal… There should be a law against men as good-looking at Alessandro Lucioni. I know the tall, dark and handsome tag is a bit of a cliché, but he's exactly that. Tall and olive-skinned, and with the sort of looks that would make any woman between the ages of fourteen and fifty throw herself on the nearest bed and beg to be ravished by him.

He has sharply chiselled cheekbones and a prominent brow that gives him a slightly intimidating air whenever he frowns. His hair is thick and plentiful and not quite short, not quite long, but somewhere fashionably in between. He looks like one of those dishy European aftershave models. That day his hair was brushed back off his forehead, and it looked like the last time he'd done it he had used his fingers.

I wished I could stop thinking about his fingers. I was breaking out into a hot flush. I could feel it deep in my core. That subtle tensing of my girly bits as I recalled the way he had stroked me there. I pressed my knees together, but that only made it worse.

'This is the…erm…library,' I said as I pushed open the door.

He stood waiting for me to go in before him. He had excellent manners. That's another thing I have to give him. Ladies first—that's his credo. *Yikes*, why couldn't I stop thinking about sex?

I turned on my heel and walked in with my head high, waving my hand to encompass the shelves and shelves of books. 'We at Emily Sudgrove Academy pride ourselves on giving our girls a broad choice in reading material which is both age-appropriate while giving them the opportunity in which to extend their reading range.'

I sounded like I was reading it from the school information booklet—which is not surprising since I was the one who rewrote the latest edition.

'Jem.'

I get called by my name, or at least the shortened version of it, all the time. There was no reason why my legs should suddenly feel as if the bones had been taken out. Or for my heart to beat extra quickly and my chest to feel tight, as if something rapidly expanding had taken up all the space in there. But something about the way Alessandro said my name made the base of my spine tingle.

I took a slow deep breath and turned to face him with my Key Stage One teacher face on. My sister Bertie calls it my Miss Prim and Proper face. Apparently I've been doing it since I was a little kid, which is kind of ironic since nothing about our childhood was anywhere close to being prim and proper.

'Miss Clark,' I said, with a tight smile that didn't reveal my teeth. 'We at Emily Sudgrove believe in teaching our girls proper forms of address, so as to equip them with the necessary tools to—'

'Why did you run away the other week in London?'

I tried to keep my expression composed. I hadn't realised he'd seen me that day. It made me cringe to think he'd witnessed my panicked bolt via the kitchen of the restaurant Bertie and I had been lunching in. But I hated seeing him with his lovers, either in the press or in the flesh. He was in and out of relationships like a cab driver in and out of his cab. I swear to God he should have a revolving door in his bedroom. Or a ticketing machine—like the ones in the deli to keep people from jumping the queue.

'I'm afraid I have no idea what you're talking about,' I said. 'You must have mistaken someone else for me.'

The corner of his mouth tipped up in a knowing smile. It was only a slight hitch of his lips but it was enough to set my pulse racing.

'I could never mistake you for anyone else, *cara mio.*'

This time I didn't bother with the composed expression. I frowned. I glared. I bristled. 'Do *not* call me that. It's Miss Clark.'

The hitch of his lips went higher, as if he found my stand-off amusing. 'How long have you been teaching here?' he asked.

I made an effort to relax my shoulders. *Keep it cool and professional.* I could do this as long as I forgot about our history. 'Five years.'

His brows moved together over his dark eyes. 'Since Paris, then?'

Paris. The city of love.

Yeah, right. The city of bitter disappointment, if you ask me. I hate Paris now. I can't even bring myself to look at a baguette without wanting to throw up or hit someone over the head with it. Or both.

I brought up my chin. 'I was ready for a change.'

His frown had melted away as if it had never been, but I got the feeling he was thinking about our time together. Shuffling through the memories like someone searching for something in a long neglected drawer. I could see the distant look in his gaze. I got the same look in mine if I allowed myself to think of that whirlwind month in Paris.

But then he blinked and rearranged his features into a cool mask. 'I chose this school because it's close to where I live.'

My heart gave a lurch. 'You live nearby?'

'I've bought a property in the countryside, just outside of Bath,' he said.

'Then why are you boarding your niece?'

'It's being renovated at present,' he said. 'I don't think it's a safe place for a young child.'

'So what will you do once it is?' I asked. 'Take her to live with you? Or will you be too busy travelling back and forth to London?' *And sleeping with anyone with a pulse*, I wanted to add but didn't.

He'd selected a book from the bookshelves and was turning it over in his hands. It was a Beatrix Potter book. My mother had a thing about Beatrix Potter. Hence Bertie's name—Beatrix, but don't call her that unless you want her to hate you—and my name. Had he chosen the book deliberately? Reminding me of the connection we'd once had?

I hadn't told him *everything* about my childhood but I'd told him a lot. Well, maybe not a lot—more like a bit. There was stuff I hadn't even told Bertie, close as we were. There were some things it was best not to talk about. Best not to even think about. I'm good at avoidance. Avoidance is my middle name... Well, it's not—but it could be.

Bertie and I don't have middle names. Our parents didn't believe in them. I suspect it's because they have about four or five apiece and can never remember them. My parents both come from aristocratic backgrounds. I figure it's a whole lot easier being a hippie when someone else is paying the bills. But don't get me started...

I watched as Alessandro slid the book back into place on the shelf. As his index fingertip slowly slid down the slim spine I felt a traitorous quake of lust roll through me. I squeezed my thighs together to stop the thrumming sensation. Like *that* was ever going to work. Just being in the same room as him was enough to make me come. That voice. Those eyes. Those hands. That delicious body...

I drank in the sight of him. The broad shoulders, the strong back and lean hips, the long legs and taut buttocks. I had run my hands and lips and tongue over every inch of that body. I had learned how to give and receive pleasure instead of being frozen with fear. A fear I hadn't told him about. Well, not the truth, anyway.

I told him my first time had been 'a bit unpleasant'. I didn't go into the details of exactly *how* unpleasant. I refuse to see myself as a victim. I don't even see myself as a survivor. I'm a fighter. I'm strong and tough and I take no crap from anyone.

Alessandro turned and his gaze locked with mine. 'You look good, Jem.'

That's another thing I hate. Compliments. I never believe them.

I've never considered myself beautiful. Even though I'm blonde and blue-eyed and slim, with a decent set of boobs—who I am to talk about clichés?—I have hang-ups about my looks. I've got my father's nose and my mother's cheekbones. I've got my maternal grandmother's hair and my paternal grandfather's chin. I don't know whose eyes I've got, but I sure hope they can see without them! Seriously, it's like all the bad bits of everyone in my family were cobbled together to make me. Thanks a bunch, God, or whoever it is in charge of genetics.

Bertie's the beautiful one in our family—not that she thinks so or anything. She would say I'm the good-looking one, but that's because she's a sweetheart. She has gorgeous brown hair and brown eyes, and the cutest smile with tiny dimples. When I smile it looks more like a grimace.

I have to remind myself that's it okay to show my teeth because for most of my childhood my teeth were like a picket fence. They were so wide apart I could have flossed with hessian rope. My parents went through a 'no medical intervention' phase, which unfortunately included dentistry. They believed my teeth would eventually find their rightful position all by themselves. Well, let me tell you they didn't. I had to endure braces and a night-time plate for three and a half years during my late teens and early adulthood. Yes. *Three and a half years!*

God, talk about excruciating torture—socially *and* physically. No wonder my sex life was a little on the barren side when I met Alessandro. Not that I cared about it all that much then—or now. If I remove my memory of Alessandro's lovemaking—which is darn near impossible to do—I think sex is horribly overrated.

I shrugged off his compliment like I did everyone

else's. 'I'll show you the boarding house. Please come this way.'

I led the way out of the library, but before I could get through the door he put a hand on my arm. I was wearing a silk shirt and a cotton cardigan, but even so I could feel the heat of his long fingers as they wrapped around my wrist like a set of handcuffs. I looked at his hand on my wrist like someone would look at a cockroach on a piece of cake. I brought my gaze up to his. How had I forgotten how tall he was? I was going to have get myself a decent set of heels or a neck brace.

'Do you mind?' I said, with a crisp note to my voice. Bertie calls it my schoolmarm tone.

His fingers didn't budge. If anything I thought they tightened a fraction. I lost myself for a moment in the bottomless depths of his coal-black gaze. I could feel his eyes drawing me in, like a magnet does a piece of metal. I could even feel my body leaning towards him, as if an unseen force was pushing me from behind.

Hell's bells. I'm starting to sound like my mother, with her paranormal take on things. She would have a field day with his aura. He was sending off vibes even I could read. Although his eyes were dark and inscrutable it felt like he was watching me from behind a closed door that had once been open.

But hadn't I always felt that way about him? He had shadows in his eyes I had chosen to ignore five years ago. I hadn't liked to press him because I knew how awful it was to talk about stuff you didn't want to talk about. I figured that, him being an orphan and all—how had I fallen for *that* lie?—meant he wasn't comfortable talking about his childhood.

Why had he lied to me? What sort of family did

he come from? Surely it couldn't be half as weird and wacky as mine.

Alessandro's thumb found my leaping pulse. *Damn.* No way of hiding that involuntary reaction from him. It didn't matter how determined I was in my brain to armour up, because he could always find a way to ambush my senses. That was why I'd so assiduously avoided him over the years. I didn't go to places I knew he frequented. I didn't want to run into him like we were old friends. Making polite conversation, talking about the weather or current affairs, as if he *hadn't* torn my heart out of my chest and ground it under the heel of one of his handmade Italian leather shoes.

I had way more self-respect than that. *No second chances* was another credo of mine. One strike and you're out. You don't get to screw over Jem Clark more than once.

I suppressed a shiver as his thumb began a slow stroke, back and forth, making every nerve beneath my skin shiver and shriek out for more. He had a mesmerising touch, gentle and yet strong. Confident. Assured. As if he knew my body like a maestro knows his favourite instrument.

Actually, it was a pretty accurate analogy, because I was as strung up as an over-tuned violin. I could feel every nerve and muscle in my body pulling taut. My insides practically shuddered with longing.

How could he possibly have that effect on me after all this time? I hated him for how he'd used me. I detested his smooth-talking artifice. Saying he wanted to spend the rest of his life with me when all he'd wanted to do was send a message to his stunningly beautiful ex that he'd moved on.

Why had I been so dumb as to fall for that? I wasn't proud of my history for falling for charming lies. The event during my early teens which I refuse to mention came about because of my naivety when it came to men and their lies.

But I'm older and wiser now. Tough as old goat's knees, that's me. No one can charm me nowadays—which is kind of why I haven't been out on a date in years. I don't care if men are put off by me. I'm fine with it. I don't want the fairy tale, like my sister. I'm not hankering after some guy to lock me away in the suburbs with two-point-five kids and a mortgage.

Besides, I have more than enough kids to take care of at school. Mothering at a distance. I can handle that. I'm darn good at it too.

I unpeeled Alessandro's fingers as I gave him a look of utter contempt. 'I don't think you heard me, Dr Lucioni.'

Dr Lucioni? Snort. Who was I kidding? No amount of formality was going to wipe away the memory of our affair. It was a presence in the room.

Sheesh. There I went with the paranormal thing again. But really—it was. I felt the erotic tension in the air like a singing wire. The memories of how we were together were swirling around inside my head. From behind the wall of my resolve I caught glimpses of our bodies locked together in passion. Rocking together, straining, writhing, climbing the summit of human pleasure until we both came apart. His long, tanned hairy legs entwined intimately with mine. His arms wrapped around me, holding me to him as if he never wanted to let me go. His mouth…

I should *not* have thought about his mouth. His mouth

had wreaked such havoc on my senses. He had used his mouth in ways I had not experienced before. No one had ever pleasured me that way. I hadn't allowed them to. But with him it had felt natural. Damn it, it had felt like he was worshipping my body. It had added a level of sanctity to our lovemaking that was sadly lacking in my past experiences...especially the one I refuse to mention.

Alessandro gave me one of his half smiles—a twitch of his lips that was borderline mocking. 'You think you can erase what we had?'

I rubbed at my wrist as if it had been stung, glaring at him so hard my eyes hurt. 'I would appreciate it if you would refrain from referring to our...association whilst within the parameters of this school.'

I sounded so priggish I almost laughed out loud. Bertie would have been doubled over at me.

His eyes took on a glint that did serious damage to my equilibrium—if indeed I had any in the first place, which I suspect I didn't.

'I've told my niece we're old friends,' he said. 'I thought it would help her to feel less threatened by coming here.'

I widened my eyes. I'm not talking cup-and-saucer wide. I'm talking satellite-dish wide, like those ones on the International Space Station.

'What?'

'You have a problem with making a small child feel a little more secure?'

I whooshed out a stormy breath. 'I have a problem with you fabricating a relationship between us that doesn't exist.'

'It did once.'

I sent him another death-adder stare. 'I beg to differ. How can you stand there and say we had something together when you failed to mention the fact that you'd recently broken up with your gold-digging fiancée? Not to mention your lies about not having a family. You lied to me from day one, Alessandro.'

I mentally kicked myself for using his Christian name. It was too personal. Too informal. Too intimate.

'You have a sister and a niece and God knows who else. That's not what people in a relationship do. They share stuff. Important stuff.'

I felt a teeny-weeny twinge of guilt at my statement. I hadn't told him *my* important stuff, but I refused to see it as important. It was not worth thinking about. I *hated* thinking about it. It gave me nightmares to think about it. It was so long ago. I had packed away the sickening memories behind layers of I'm-a-tough-girl-don't-mess-with-me bravado.

'I would've told you in time.'

I rolled my eyes in disdain. 'Like when?' I said. 'On our fiftieth wedding anniversary?'

Ack! There's another word I loathe. Wedding.

'But there wasn't going to *be* a wedding, was there? Or even an engagement. Our quick-fire affair was all for show. After you'd achieved your aim of royally annoying your ex you would've neatly extricated yourself from our—' I put my fingers up in air quotation marks '—"relationship" and moved on to your next conquest. You're just annoyed I saw through you and got out first.'

His eyes held mine in a dark, unreadable lock. 'I'm not here to talk about the past. I'm here to talk about my niece's future.'

I gave him a narrow look. 'Why this school?'

His eyes didn't waver as they held mine. 'I told you. It's convenient for where I'll be living.'

'So you're thinking of settling down at some point?'

Why are you asking that? I thought. *You. Do. Not. Care.*

'At some point.'

I was like a dog with a bone. A terrier, that's me. Now I had him here I wanted to know everything— even the stuff I didn't want to know. Maybe it wasn't a bone I was hanging on to. It was a smelly old carcass I was rolling in.

'Are you in a relationship with someone at present?' I said.

'No.'

'What about the blonde the other week?'

His eyes glinted as if in triumph. 'Was that your sister with you?'

I glowered at him. Why had I allowed myself to fall into his trap so easily? But then, I thought, what was the point in denying I'd seen him? It was making me look foolish, and the last thing I wanted was to appear foolish and gauche in front of him.

'Yes. Who was your date?'

'The practice manager from my consulting rooms.'

I only just managed to stop myself from rolling my eyes. I could just imagine the 'practice' they'd get up to.

'I'd love to see her job description.'

His jaw tensed as if he found my comment irritating. 'It was her birthday. Now, let's get on with the tour, shall we?'

It annoyed me that he'd made me look petty and unprofessional. 'This way,' I said, and turned smartly on my heels.

But I was all too acutely aware of his tall, commanding frame following close behind.

CHAPTER TWO

I COULD SMELL the lemon and spice of his aftershave as I led the way to the dormitories on the second floor. It was a subtle scent, redolent of warm summer afternoons in a lemon grove. I thought of that brief time in Paris—the way we'd met by accident when I'd run into him as I was coming out of a shop late on a Saturday afternoon. He steadied me with his hands and I looked up into his face and my heart all but stopped.

I'm the last person who would ever believe in love at first sight, but something happened at that moment I still can't explain. I felt something shift inside me as his dark brown eyes met mine. He spoke to me in fluent French, so that might have explained it. It made me fall all the faster. And then he was so gallant, bending down to help me pick up the tote bag that had slipped off my shoulder, spilling its contents all over the cobblestones.

When he handed me my wand of lip gloss our fingers touched. I felt a fizzing sensation that travelled all the way up my arm and somehow ended in a molten pool between my legs.

He led me to a quiet table in the shade of a leafy tree outside a café on the Rue de Seine and ordered sparkling mineral water for me and an espresso for himself. We talked for two hours but it felt like two minutes.

He told me how he had grown up in Sicily but had studied and trained in London, and was spending that year working at Paris's top cardiac centre to complete his PhD before heading back to London. Most surgeons found the specialty hard enough, but he'd taken on even more study.

He fascinated me. I was spellbound by his warm, intelligent brown eyes and his long-fingered hands that had so briefly touched mine. I thought of those hands, how they performed intricate surgery and saved countless lives. I sat there aching for him to touch me again. I must have communicated it silently, for he suddenly reached across the table and took my hand in his, stroking his thumb over the back of it as his eyes meshed with mine.

He didn't have to say a word. I could see it in his gaze. I knew it was the same in mine. There was a connection between us that transcended the primal attraction of two healthy consenting adults. I had never felt a surge of lust so overpowering, and yet I could feel something else as well, which was less easily defined.

Looking back, I suspect I recognised some quality in him that spoke to the lonely outsider in me, which I prided myself on keeping well hidden. My mother would say it was fate, or kismet, or the planets aligning or something. My father would say it had something to do with our chakras being balanced. Whatever it was, the world seemed to carry on without us as we sat there gazing into each other's eyes.

I gave myself a mental slap and pushed open the first dormitory door. 'We sleep the Key Stage One and

Two girls two to a room to encourage close friendship,' I said. 'The older girls can request single rooms, but we encourage sharing to maintain a sense of family.'

Alessandro gave the dormitory a cursory look before meeting my gaze. I wondered if he could see any trace of the nostalgia that had momentarily sideswiped me. His eyes moved back and forth between each of mine as if searching for something.

'Are you happy, *ma petite*?'

I felt my knees weaken at the French endearment. I covered it quickly by pasting a poised and professional look on my face. I could *not* allow myself to be lured back into his sensual orbit. His voice, no matter what language he spoke—French, Italian, English or a combination of all three—made a frisson of delight shimmy down my spine.

I wondered if my voice had the same effect on him. Not flipping likely. I might have smoothed over my Yorkshire vowels after years of living in London, but even so there was no way anyone would want to listen to me reading the phone directory.

'What's wrong with Claudia's mother?' I asked, to steer the conversation away from my emotional health.

An impenetrable sheen came over his eyes and he turned away to look at the dormitory, with its two neatly made beds and the waist-high bookshelf that doubled as a bedside table between. There were two teddy bears in pink and purple tutus sitting side by side on the top. It might have been any bedroom in the suburbs except for the sound of schoolchildren playing in the playground outside.

'She's receiving treatment for a protracted illness,' he said after a long moment.

Something in my stomach slipped. 'Terminal?'

'I hope not.'

I bit my lip as I thought of six-year-old Claudia losing her mother. My mother—both my parents, actually—drove me nuts, but I couldn't imagine not having her around any more.

What would it do to a little girl so young to have no one but her uncle to watch out for her? Who would help her with the issues of growing up? Who would tell her about the birds and the bees, not to mention the blowflies who could destroy her innocence in…? Well, I'm not going to go there. Who would she turn to when the world seemed to be against her? Or when she got her heart broken for the first time? Who would hold her and tell her they loved her more than life itself?

'What about Claudia's father?' I asked.

Alessandro's top lip developed an unmistakable curl of disdain. 'He's not in the picture. Never has been. Claudia has never met him.'

'What about grandparents?'

The line of his mouth tightened until it was almost flat. 'There are none on either side.'

None? Or none he wanted to acknowledge? I wondered. 'Why didn't you tell me you had a sister five years ago?' I said.

He drew in a deep breath and slowly released it. I watched as his broad shoulders went down on the long exhale and what looked like a tiny flicker of pain passed over his features.

'We weren't in contact at that point.'

'Why?'

'It's complicated.'

'It sounds it.'

He gave me a level look. 'It's important to me that Claudia settles in as quickly and seamlessly as possible.'

'What have you told her about her mother's illness?'

He held my gaze for a moment before he looked away again. He let out another long breath. 'Not much. I didn't want her overburdened with worry about things she can't change. She's a sensitive child.'

'Then she'll join the dots for herself but probably come up with the wrong picture,' I said. 'You should be honest with her. Kids are much more resilient than you realise.'

His eyes collided again with mine, one of his brows going up in an arc. '*Are* they?'

It was a pointed question that hung suspended in the air.

I found myself going back in time to my own childhood, thinking of all the times when a bit of resilience would have come in handy. My parents' hippie lifestyle was fine for them, but it hadn't been fine for me or for my younger sister Bertie. So many times I'd had to take on a parenting role for Bertie's sake because our parents were missing in action, so to speak.

It's not that they weren't loving parents—if anything they were too indulgent. We didn't have any proper boundaries—not just to keep us in line, but also to give others a clear message that someone was watching out for us. Mum and Dad were dreamers—drifters who never stayed in one place long enough to put down roots—which meant Bertie and I had little stability during our childhood. We would no sooner make friends at one place before we'd be shuffled on to another location where some visionary guru was setting up a new lifestyle commune our parents were keen to join.

I was always watching out for Bertie, who got bullied a lot. I did too, until I learned to stand up for myself. I had to pretend to be tougher than I really was in order to survive. It's a good skill to have, but it has its downside. After all those years of playing tough it's hard to find my soft centre. It's been bricked in, like a vault cemented into a wall. I don't know if you can call that resilience or not.

I stopped thinking about my childhood and started speculating on Alessandro's. Was that why he had posed the question? Was there something about *his* childhood that made him sceptical of a child's ability to cope with what life dished up? I had always seen him as a strong, invincible sort of person. He had brushed off his 'orphan' status with a casual it-happened-a-long-time-ago-and-I'm-over-it shrug. But what had made him pretend to be alone in the world?

I didn't think it had been to garner sympathy. He was too self-reliant to want or need anyone else's comfort. That was what I'd found so attractive about him. He didn't care what people thought of him other than in a professional sense. He'd told me he wasn't out to win a popularity contest but to save lives. He got on with his life as if other people's opinions were irrelevant.

I secretly envied him as I'd spent so much of my life trying to fit in. I'd learned to morph into whatever I needed to be in order to belong. My chameleon-like behaviour had turned me into someone I didn't always like, but I wasn't sure how to go back to being the warm and friendly and open girl I had once been. To be perfectly honest, I wasn't sure if I even wanted to be that girl any more. That girl had got herself into trouble, and the last thing I wanted to attract was trouble.

Alessandro might have been in any sort of career and I would still have been attracted to him. I had been totally swept away by him—charmed and captivated by his take-charge, can-do attitude, which was so at odds with the way I had been raised. He was goal-orientated and disciplined. He didn't dream or drift aimlessly, or wait for someone else to tell him what he should do. He made plans and set about fulfilling them. He hadn't let his background or lack of family money stop him from becoming one of London's top heart specialists. He had laid down a career path as a young boy and got on with making it happen.

His intelligence was the biggest turn-on for me. I don't mean his doctor status, because that sort of thing doesn't impress me. I loved it that he was well read and well informed on topics I had barely even thought of before. But it was the physical intensity between us that took me completely by surprise. I had never considered myself a sensual person. The event I refuse to talk about put paid to that when I was thirteen. I wasn't the touchy-feely sort. I didn't hug or kiss. I didn't seek affection and I didn't give it—unless there was no avoiding it, like at Christmas and on birthdays.

But with Alessandro I embraced my sexuality. I celebrated my womanhood with every cell of my body. I bloomed and burned and blazed under his touch. I discovered things about my body I had no idea it was capable of—wickedly delightful things that left my skin tingling for hours afterwards. I loved exploring the hard contours of Alessandro's body. I just about crawled into his skin once I lost my first flutter of fear.

I had never seen a man more beautifully made. Although I'm not a doctor like my sister Bertie, who sees

naked men all the time, I've seen a few. My parents
went through a naturalist stage when I was in my early
teens, so the male form is no stranger to me. Talk about
embarrassing… Most of those men had the sort of bodies one would think they would be desperate to cover
up with clothes—layers and layers of them. But, no, it
was all out on show. However, none of the men I had
seen in their birthday suits had looked anywhere as perfect as Alessandro. He wasn't gym-obsessed perfect,
but rather healthy and virile and in-his-prime perfect.

I had to give myself another mental slap to keep my
mind on the conversation. Images of his naked body
were flooding my brain to such a degree I could feel
warmth blooming in my cheeks. I rarely blush. I lost my
innocence a long time ago. But something about Alessandro's penetrating gaze made me feel as if he could
see exactly where my mind was taking me.

I realised then with a little jolt that the intimacy we'd
shared would always be between us. We had 'A History'.
It wasn't as if I could wipe it away, like I do the day's
lesson from the whiteboard in the classroom. There was
a permanent record of it in my flesh.

I was tattooed with his touch, indelibly marked, so
that when any other man touched me I automatically
compared it to Alessandro's and found it sadly lacking.
It's basically why I haven't bothered dating. I don't see
the point. Quite frankly, I could do without being reminded I'm basically dead from the waist down with
anyone else.

'I'll…erm…show you the bathrooms,' I said, and
made to turn away.

But his hand stalled me again. I had folded my arms
across my body, which meant his hand was tantalisingly

close to my breasts. I felt the stirring tingle of my flesh, as if my breasts had picked up his proximity like some sort of finely tuned radar.

My breath stalled somewhere in the middle of my throat. I brought my gaze up to his. His eyes were so dark it was impossible to make out his pupils. A girl could get lost in those eyes. Disappear and never be found again.

My gaze went to his mouth as if of its own volition. My stomach did a rollercoaster loop and drop as I recalled how his lips had felt against mine. The taste of him, the feel of him, the sensual power of him had made everything so tight and bound up inside me unwind. His lips were evenly shaped—neither too thick or too thin. He had shaved that morning, but even so I could see the urgent pinpricks of stubble surrounding his mouth and on his lean jaw.

My fingers twitched to slide over it, to remind myself of the erotic feel of his prickly male skin against the softness my female flesh.

I dragged in a ragged breath and brought my gaze back to his, but he was now looking at *my* mouth, a small frown tugging at his brow. I ran the tip of my tongue over my lips and my stomach did another crazy somersault as I saw his sexily hooded eyes follow its pathway.

I swear to God someone had sucked all the oxygen out of the air. I was finding it hard to breathe. I was standing there as if I'd been snap freeze-dried. I couldn't have move if I'd tried.

His hand reached out and ever so gently cupped my cheek. A shiver of reaction coursed through me, but for some reason I still didn't move away. It was like I was under his spell. Totally under his control, with no will to snap out of it. The pad of his thumb moved over the circle of my chin, not quite touching my lower lip but close enough for it to go into raptures of tingling, fizzing anticipation. His eyes remained focused on my mouth, as if he too were recalling how it had felt against his.

Was he going to kiss me? Would I allow him to? I was in a conundrum. I wanted to feel his mouth on mine if for no other reason than to prove to myself that I'd been imagining it had felt far more amazing than it actually had. I guess I also wanted to prove to myself that I could resist him. That I could withstand the commanding pressure of his mouth and not melt into a pool of mush.

But another shockingly traitorous part of me wanted to close the distance between our mouths and give myself up to the storm of passion I could feel building inside my body. It was surging through my blood, firing up all my senses, making me giddy with longing. A longing I could feel pounding deep in my core. The relentless ache of it was part pleasure, part pain. It had been so long since I'd felt desire I was shocked at how powerful it was.

I realised then how base I was. How utterly primal my urges were that, for all my prim and proper fastidiousness, I was as earthy and lust driven as anyone else.

Alessandro's thumb pressed against my lower lip and I all but whimpered. I smothered it as best I could but I saw the gleam of satisfaction in his eyes as they meshed with mine.

'Have dinner with me tonight,' he said.

The fact he'd issued it as a command rather than

asked me was enough to break the spell. I stepped out of his light hold and sent him an icy glare.

'The staff at Emily Sudgrove are prohibited from fraternising with the parents or guardians of the girls,' I said.

That wasn't strictly true, but it sounded like it could be. I hoped he wouldn't find out about Kate McManus, a young widow who had recently started dating our Physical Education teacher, Rob Canning. We were delighted with the budding romance, because Rob had gone through a really painful divorce a few years ago and Kate was the only woman he'd dated since.

'Are you involved with someone?' Alessandro said.

I put on my best haughty look. Bertie reckons no one can do haughty better than me. I can arch my brows and look down my nose and send sparks of scorn from my gaze like a blue-blooded aristocrat staring down an impudent underling.

'I have no idea what makes you think you have the right to ask me such an impertinently personal question, Dr Lucioni,' I said.

His mouth tipped up at one corner, as if he found me amusing rather than threatening. 'So that's a no,' he said.

I wished I could deny it, but he would only have to ask around to find out my dating track record was abysmal. My life was a cycle of work, eat and sleep. I occasionally threw in a bit of exercise to break it up a bit. But the fact is I love my job. I don't want to be distracted from it. As far as I can see, having a relationship is one big time suck.

I didn't have the time or the inclination to be someone's date for a few weeks or months, until they found someone more attractive or more interesting. I had much more important things to do with my time. I was proud of the work I did with the girls—especially the ones who struggled to fulfil their high-flying, high-achieving parents' dreams for them. I spent a lot of time planning lessons and writing up programmes and exercises.

I'm not a chalk-and-talk teacher. I'm interactive and creative and I thrive on seeing the girls in my charge blossom and play to their strengths. I would much rather give my girls an A for effort and attitude than an A for academic prowess.

My mother laments the fact that my life has no balance but who is she to talk? She hasn't held down a job since before Bertie and I were born. Nor has my father. They've lived on their parents' trust funds while meditating their mostly peaceful way around the country. I say 'mostly' because there was one occasion a couple of years back when I had to bail both of them out of a county court after a forestry expansion protest got a little ugly. It was quite a while before I could turn on the television without expecting to see an image of my parents chained to a tree, dressed in hemp clothing and waving placards.

Lately even Bertie has been banging on about me finding someone now she's got herself engaged to a fellow doctor. I must admit when I met her fiancé I did feel a teeny-weeny twinge of envy. The way Matt Bishop looked at my sister made me feel all squishy and gooey inside. But I quickly squashed the feeling. Bertie has always been a romantic, with her head in the clouds. I'm much more down to earth and practical. Believe me, I've had to be. Someone in our family had to have their head screwed on.

I pursed my lips at Alessandro. One thing I did have in common with my little sister was that I did not appreciate being laughed at.

'You find it funny that I choose to be single?' I said. '*You're* currently single, are you not?'

His brows lifted slightly. 'I didn't realise you took such an interest and followed my love-life in the press.'

I could have kicked myself. I had as good as admitted to poring over every inch of the tabloids for news of him. Mind you, he kept a much lower profile than some others of his ilk. Being a celebrity doctor and a bachelor made men like him a juicy target for the press.

Every time I saw a photo of him with some gorgeous model-type I would seethe and quake with rage. It would reopen all the wounds I'd tried so hard to heal. It was like rock salt being pummelled into them.

But why he had never settled for long with anyone since me puzzled me. The ex he had been so keen to prove a point to had married the man she'd left Alessandro for—a high-profile businessman who was super-duper wealthy. But I'd heard whispers in the press that the marriage was in trouble. Was he waiting for her to divorce her husband so they could be together?

I glowered at Alessandro as I stalked past to lead the way on the rest of the tour. I pointed out the bathrooms, and then the games room, and the juniors' and the seniors' common rooms. I spoke in a flat monotone, stripping my expression of anything other than excruciating boredom.

If he was annoyed by my little show of defiance he didn't show it on his face. His expression was mostly blank, apart from that faraway look I caught a glimpse of now and again. Finally we made our way outside into the sunshine, where the children were playing just before the lunch break ended.

One of my pupils, a little girl called Harriet, came gambolling up with a cheeky grin on her freckled face. 'Is that man your boyfriend, Miss Clark?'

I'm not one to blush easily, but right then I could feel heat spreading like a grass fire across my cheeks.

When I was a little kid I didn't think teachers were anything but teachers. I didn't think they had a personal life. To me they were like police or firemen or other authority figures. They didn't seem like real people. Not so today's kids. They know too damn much and way too early.

'No, Harriet,' I said. 'Dr Lucioni is enrolling his niece into our school. I'm giving him a guided tour.'

Harriet scrunched up her face as she peered at Alessandro. 'Are you a movie star?'

Alessandro's smile at Harriet made something at the backs of my knees go fizzy.

'No, I'm afraid not.'

Harriet wasn't convinced. 'You *look* famous.'

'Run along, Harriet,' I said. 'The bell is about to ring.'

As if I'd summoned it, the bell sounded, and Harriet scampered off to join the rest of the girls as they prepared to enter the building for the afternoon's lessons.

I turned to face Alessandro. 'That's my cue as well. When shall I expect Claudia to come to class?'

'I'll bring her tomorrow.'

'Where is she now?'

'With a temporary nanny.'

'Why didn't you bring her with you today?' I said. 'It would've helped her to get her bearings. Meeting the other girls and so on.'

His eyes tethered mine in a lock that made my insides flutter as if a handful of flustered moths were trapped in the cavity of my stomach.

'I thought it best for us to meet alone first,' he said.

I didn't think it was wise for me to *ever* be alone with him. I didn't trust myself. He had a frightening way of dismantling my self-control with a look or a casual touch. My chin was still tingling from where his thumb had stroked. My wrist was still burning as if he had left a brand on my flesh. My inner core was still pulsating with the memory of how his body had moved within mine.

Again I wondered if he was remembering all we had shared in that brief mad fling I'd stupidly thought would last for ever.

His gaze was dark and bottomless…inscrutable, enigmatic. Mesmerising.

The sound of the second end-of-lunch bell startled me out of my stasis. 'Excuse me,' I said with a formal quirk of my lips that passed for a smile. 'I have to get to class.'

He put out his hand, and because we were in full view of the school admin office, as well as Miss Fletcher's office, I had no choice but to slide mine into it.

His fingers closed around mine in the same way they had before. There was nothing formal or polite about it. It was purely erotic. Wickedly, shamelessly erotic.

I drew my hand away from the temptation of his

touch and turned and walked into the school building. But it was not until school finished that day that my hand finally stopped tingling.

CHAPTER THREE

I WAS AT SCHOOL early the next morning…earlier than usual. So shoot me. I'm a lark, not an owl. I like to get on with the day from the get-go. I bounce out of bed and hit the ground like a lightning bolt. It's because I'm a list-maker. I thrive on being organised. It's like an addiction. I even write down things I've already done, just so I can get that little buzz of satisfaction at seeing it ticked off.

My parents think I'm crazy not to start my day with some peaceful mindfulness practice or yoga poses or chanting. They sleep in until midday when they come to stay, which drives me completely nuts. And I use the term 'sleep in' loosely. They do a lot of things in bed when they come to stay, and not much of it involves sleeping.

Everyone thinks their parents don't 'do it', but my parents make sure everyone knows they do. At least these days they're only doing it with each other. Up until a couple of years ago they had an 'open relationship', which meant they could have sex with anyone they fancied and the other wouldn't mind. Bertie and I found it completely and utterly weird.

My mother is embarrassingly open about sex. My

dad too, although he doesn't drop it into every conversation like my mother does. It's the first thing she asks me when she calls. 'How's your sex life?' Or, yesterday's cracker: 'Did you know having an orgasm every day is good for your pelvic floor?'

Seriously, I think she's obsessed or something.

I like being at school early because I like being prepared. I like getting my lessons organised, with all the little extra touches I've designed that are tailor-made to each child's learning style and personality. I like watching the girls come in through the school gate or walk over from the boarding house. I guess it's my version of people-watching.

I learn a lot about the dynamic between parents and their children by watching what happens in the hand over. You can see the parents who have a tendency to do too much for their kids. They're the one carrying the kid's backpack or tennis racket or lacrosse stick or musical instrument. I have nothing against parents helping little kids with their things, but senior girls…? Honestly…

I also learn a lot about the dynamic between the girls and what sort of mood they are in as they file into the building. I can tell which girl has had a bad night, or which one is homesick, or which one is lauding it over another. I can almost read their little minds.

Maybe I'm more like my mother than I realise. Scary thought.

After a few of the regulars had arrived I noticed a shiny black sports car pull up in front of the school. A lot of expensive cars pull up in front of the Emily Sudgrove School for Girls, but this one stood out. It was a top-model Maserati, with tinted windows so you couldn't see who was behind the wheel or inside the car. It had a throaty roar I swear you'd be able to hear from the next suburb. Possibly from across the English Channel.

I watched as Alessandro got out from behind the wheel with the sort of athletic grace I privately envied. It's not that I'm clumsy or anything, but I've never mastered the art of alighting from a vehicle without showing too much leg or, on one spectacularly embarrassing occasion, my underwear—which was unfortunately not the sensible sort.

Alessandro opened the back passenger door and leaned down to speak to the little girl inside. I saw him take her by the hand and gently help her from the car. When I saw him smile at his niece a hand reached deep inside my chest and squeezed my heart. He gave Claudia's ponytail a little tug and then led her by the hand towards the entrance of school, carrying a suitcase, presumably full of her belongings, in the other.

When we'd been together Alessandro had spoken openly about his desire for a family. I'd been ecstatic. So many men were either not ready or didn't want kids at all. I was so thrilled that I'd found a man who wanted the things I wanted. Back then I wanted to have kids and do all the things with them my parents hadn't done with Bertie and I.

I wanted to live with them in a proper house—not a commune or a tree house or a bark hut. I wanted to toilet train them instead of letting them go wherever or whenever nature called. Don't ask, but rest assured I'd sorted it out by the time I was four and taught Bertie in the process. I wanted to be interested in their education, supervising it so they got the help and encouragement they needed. I wanted to go on holidays—not communal ones, with a guru dictating the programme, but relaxing ones where I could play with my kids and enjoy the magic of their childhood.

And I wanted to share the whole experience with a man I loved and trusted to stand by me no matter what.

Yeah, I know. What a deluded fool I was.

I was waiting in my classroom, pretending to be sorting out flashcards, when Alessandro arrived at the door. I put the flashcards down and smiled at the little girl standing meekly by his side.

'Hello, Claudia,' I said, and squatted down so we were eye to eye. 'My name is Miss Clark. It's lovely to have you in my class.'

Claudia had the biggest brown eyes I'd ever seen, fringed with thick lashes that were like miniature black fans. Her skin was olive toned but quite pale, as if she spent a lot of time indoors. She was small for her age, delicate and finely made, with thin wrists and ankles, and she had a pretty little cupid's bow mouth that was currently finding it difficult to smile.

'Go on, Claudia,' Alessandro prompted gently. 'Say hello to Miss Clark.'

Claudia's little cheeks turned bright red and she bent her chin to her chest as she mumbled so softly I could barely hear her. 'Hello, Mith C-C-C-C-Clark.'

My heart gave another painful squeeze when I heard that shy little voice with its lisp and stutter. It reminded me of myself at that age, when I had a terrible speech impediment. I was mercilessly teased about it.

There are times when I can still hear the mean kids imitating my inability to say certain words. Anything starting with a hard-sounding consonant was torture for me. I finally got control of it by the time I was ten—and not because my parents sent me to a speech therapist. They flatly refused to. They believed my stutter was a voice from one of my past lives trying to be heard and that I had to be patient and allow them to channel through me. *Yeah, right.* Why is it that everyone's been a prince or princess in a past life and never a penniless pauper?

Anyway, back to my stutter. It was because of a teacher I had—once we were placed back in school—who was really fabulous at teaching drama. She used to give me the best roles to play and like magic my stutter would disappear. It was as if by playing someone else I could forget about my speech impediment. I've since done a special education diploma in language and learning difficulties, which I've found enormously helpful as a classroom teacher.

I straightened so I could speak to Alessandro. I had to keep my friendly and open smile in place, but it nearly killed me.

'There's just enough time for me to take Claudia over to the boarding house to meet the house mistress,' I said. 'It would be good to get her settled in before class starts. Her roommate, Phoebe Milton, is looking forward to meeting her.'

A pleated frown appeared between his eyes. 'You're right. I should've thought of that yesterday. But there's been so much to do over the last few days.'

I realised then that looking after a small child of six was a probably a relatively new experience for him. He was out of his depth and doing everything he could not to show it. It made me feel a flicker of compassion for him I wasn't expecting to feel. I didn't want to feel a flicker of *anything* for him, but seeing him with his little niece took the sharp edges off my bitterness—like a file does a ragged fingernail.

He was so kind and tender and protective of her. He hadn't once let go of her tiny hand. Just seeing his large tanned hand gently holding that tiny pale one made my heart contract again. There was so much I wanted to ask him, but with his little charge there to hear every word I had to hold my tongue. I also didn't want to let little Claudia pick up on anything untoward between Alessandro and I.

He had already said she was a sensitive child and I could well believe it. Her obvious shame at her lisp and her stutter was making my chest ache with sympathy so badly it hurt every time I took a breath. It would be irresponsible of me, not to mention unprofessional, to give Claudia the impression I was at odds with her uncle—even though it was true. From what I'd gathered so far, he was the only anchor she had right now.

Once we got to the boarding house I introduced Alessandro and Claudia to Jennifer Lancaster, the boarding-house mistress. Once pleasantries were exchanged, Jennifer took Claudia by the hand and showed her where she would be sleeping.

'How long has Claudia been with you?' I asked Alessandro, once we were out of his niece's hearing.

'Two weeks.'

Yikes, I thought. That would certainly have put the brakes on his playboy lifestyle.

'You mentioned you'd lost contact with Claudia's mother,' I said. 'How long have you been back in contact?'

'About a month,' he said. 'She called me out of the blue and said she needed my help.'

I sent him a sideways glance but he was looking at his niece, who was standing quietly as Jennifer unpacked her belongings. Claudia was biting down on her bottom lip, and even though we were a few feet away I could see the distinct wobble of her little chin.

'Should I go to her?' he asked, turning to look at me.

I was tempted to bite my own lip in sympathy for the poor little kid. But I knew from experience that drawing too much attention to the imminent separation of parent/guardian and child sometimes made it worse.

'The first couple of days will be hard, but she'll soon settle in,' I said. 'Jennifer's put her with a lovely little kid. They'll be best friends before you know it.'

Fortunately Phoebe came in at that point, so the two girls had a chance to meet before class. Phoebe was as ebullient as a friendly puppy, thankfully doing enough of the talking for Claudia simply to stand there and smile shyly.

'At least it's not for long,' Alessandro said as he and I watched the two girls interact. 'I hope to have the house ready in a month, tops.'

Was it the dream house we had talked about while lying in bed in Paris on those wonderful mornings when I'd basked in the glow of his lovemaking? Who would he share it with now? A knife stabbed me under the ribs. Why couldn't I move on? So what if he found someone to have babies with? I. Did. Not. Care.

'How long do you think you'll have Claudia?' I asked.

'It depends on how my sister responds to treatment.' He turned and looked at me again. 'I would appreciate it if you'd call me immediately if you have any concerns about my niece.' He handed me a business card with his contact details on it. 'You can call me any time. Day or night.'

I pocketed the card as Jennifer came over with Claudia and Phoebe, who were holding hands.

'Ready to meet the rest of your classmates?' I said with a bright, enthusiastic smile.

Claudia gave a tiny nod without speaking, her big soulful eyes making that knife under my ribs jab a little harder.

'How's your new pupil settling in?' asked Lucy Gatton, the Reception/Kindergarten class teacher, when I came into the staffroom at lunchtime.

I gave Lucy a brief rundown on what I'd observed about Claudia and her speech impediment, and the way she compensated for it by allowing others to speak for her.

'She's a little on the shy side, but she seems to be fitting in without too much trouble,' I said. 'Phoebe Milton's taken her under her wing.'

I could have kissed Phoebe for how brilliantly she was looking after Alessandro's niece. Phoebe's parents were missionaries in Sierra Leone. She had been sent to England with her brother to be educated after an Ebola virus outbreak a few months ago. I was amazed at how easily she had adapted to boarding school. It was as if she was on her own little mission—taking care of the natives, so to speak. She was a born nurturer who was always on the watch for anyone who needed a bit of love and care.

She reminded me of Bertie at that age—always eager

to please and friendly to a fault—and I was hopeful that Claudia and Phoebe would become best buddies once Claudia developed some confidence. It was only the first day and the poor little munchkin had been through a lot just recently.

It's hard as a teacher not to become emotionally involved. *Too* emotionally involved, I mean. The kids feel like *my* kids. I want to protect them like a mother hen. I hate seeing them struggle. I feel actual physical pain when I see them cry or hurt themselves or get hurt by others. I could tell Claudia was going to be one of those kids I would be lying awake at night worrying about. She had a haunted look in those big brown eyes—as if she'd seen things no child of her age should ever have seen.

'Was that her father who brought her to school?' Lucy asked.

'No, her uncle.'

I could feel the probe of Lucy's gaze as I set about making myself a cup of tea. I had tried to keep my expression suitably composed when dealing with Alessandro earlier, but anyone who knew anything about body language would have known I wasn't entirely at ease with him. Half the time my body had been giving off signals I had absolutely no control over.

How was I going to maintain a professional standing when he was around? How much would he *be* around? Although Claudia was boarding at Emily Sudgrove it was solely for practical reasons. Would he come and visit her regularly? How was I going to avoid him? At the very least there would be the parent-teacher interviews, which we do twice a term—more frequently if there's a problem.

And the more I saw of little Claudia the more I realised there *was* a problem...

'He looks kind of familiar...' Lucy tapped her chin
for a moment. 'Of *course*! He's that celebrity doctor,
isn't he? I didn't recognise him, dressed in civvies. I
saw a couple of press interviews but he was wearing
scrubs. He's gorgeous looking, isn't he?'

'Is he?' I reached for a tea bag from the box on the
shelf. 'I hadn't noticed.'

Lucy gave a snorting laugh. 'Pull the other one, Jem.
Tell you what—I wish one of *my* uncles looked like
him. Is he single?'

'Apparently.' I spent an inordinate amount of time
jiggling the tea bag in my cup.

'So how come he's looking after his niece?' Lucy
asked.

'Her mother's ill.'

'Cancer?'

'He didn't say, and I didn't like to pry,' I said. 'I got
the feeling it was painful for him to discuss.'

'Poor little kid.' Lucy sighed. 'But is boarding school
the right place for her?'

'Al—Dr Lucioni is renovating his house,' I said, just
catching myself from saying his Christian name in time.
'Claudia will live with him once it's completed, or until
her mother is out of hospital—whichever happens first.'

'But if the kid's mother's in hospital and she's boarding he won't be able to take her to see her.'

I'd been thinking the very same thing. Years ago no
one took children to visit their loved ones in hospital in
the belief that it would terrify them or make them too
upset. It was the same with funerals. Children were kept
away in an effort to shield them. But children needed to

process the same emotions that adults felt, with plenty of support at hand.

'I know,' I said to Lucy. 'I guess he thinks it's for the best. Perhaps the mother's on a ventilator or something. That would be pretty distressing to see as a little kid.'

'Maybe she's in a psych ward?' Lucy said.

A ghostly hand touched the back of my neck with icy fingers. Was that why Alessandro was keeping his little niece away? Was Claudia's mother mentally unstable?

Mental illness is possibly the most difficult of all conditions for a child to understand. The impact of medication can often make things worse before it makes things better. It's harrowing for everyone involved, let alone a small child who looks to their parent for safety and security.

I frowned into my cup and saw the tea-leaves had spilled out of the tea bag from all the jiggling. They'd made a weird swirly pattern on the bottom of my cup.

I couldn't help wondering what my mother would make of it.

I stayed late at school—there was nothing unusual in that—to check that Claudia was settling in to the boarding house. I found her and Phoebe sitting on the floor of their bedroom with a bunch of Barbies in various states of dress and undress.

I didn't interrupt them for long. As usual Phoebe was doing all the talking, but Claudia was handing her articles of clothing and tiny high-heeled shoes, and seemed to be enjoying herself. I suspected Phoebe's friendly chatter relaxed Claudia as it took the pressure off her to speak. After all, there are speakers and there are listeners. Some people are much more comfortable doing all the talking. Others like to take time to listen and reflect. I suspected that even without her speech impediment Claudia would still be a reserved and reflective child.

On the way out I had a chat with Jennifer to make sure everything was going fine, and was reassured to hear Claudia had eaten a healthy after-school snack and had even smiled a couple of times at something Phoebe had said. I wondered if the boarding house was providing the sort of security and routine Claudia might have been missing in her life with her mother. I couldn't let it go. I *had* to find out what was wrong with her mother.

But the only way I could do that was to meet with Alessandro. In private.

I found his address on the school's computer system. I had his number on the business card he'd given me, but I didn't want to give him a heads-up about me coming to visit. I wanted simply to show up. I know it was cynical of me, but I wanted to cold-call him to see if he really *was* renovating—not trying to keep some sexy little model-type a secret while his little niece languished at boarding school.

I know. I'm a hard case. But it's his fault.

I drove about twenty minutes out of Bath into the countryside that makes England so famous. Verdant rolling fields, birds twittering in the hedgerows and late-afternoon sunlight casting everything in a golden hue that looked as picturesque as a postcard.

I turned up a tree-lined driveway that had a creamy-coloured Georgian mansion at the end of it. The trees' overarching limbs with their fresh spring growth created a lime-green canopy overhead. It was like driving through a long, leafy tunnel.

The mansion, on closer inspection, was indeed in the

throes of being renovated. Tradesmen's tools such as ladders and sawhorses and scaffolding surrounded the building, and stonemasons had clearly been doing their thing. However, they weren't currently doing their thing as it was way past knock-off time. The place looked deserted.

I parked the car and got out, waiting for a sign of anyone responding to my arrival. Not that my car gave anything like the roar Alessandro's had done outside school that morning. My car is more of the coughing and spluttering type, although today was a good day. So far.

I stood there for five minutes... Well, it was probably closer to thirty seconds, but it felt like five years. In case you haven't already guessed by now, I'm not the most patient person on the planet.

I walked across the gravel courtyard to the front door, my footsteps sounding like I was walking over bubble wrap in spiky heels. There was a brass doorbell on the left-hand side of the door, which I noted needed a good polish. It made no sound at all that I could tell from where I was standing. I gave the door a rap with my knuckles but—unlike in all those period dramas my sister loves watching—no uniformed butler answered my summons.

I looked at the door for a moment before reaching out and turning the doorknob. The door opened with a ghostly creak that made the hairs on the back of my neck stand up. The sensible, law-abiding side of my brain was asking, *What the hell are you doing trespassing on private property?* But the other side was saying, *Go on. Have a good old snoop. You know you want to.*

I stepped over the threshold and peered around in

the failing light. Thousands of dust motes were floating in the air, as if my entry had disturbed them from a century-long slumber. I stepped further inside, and the floorboards announced my presence with a screech of protest. It gave me such a fright that I let go of the doorknob and a tiny gust of wind—it might even have been a ghost, but don't tell my mother I said that—closed the door behind me with a snap that sounded as loud as a rifle shot.

My heart was suddenly not where it was supposed to be. It had leapt from my chest to my throat and was fluttering there like a pigeon stuck in a pipe. I gave myself a good old talking-to and reached for the doorknob. It wouldn't budge. I rattled it a couple of times. I turned it this way and that. I tugged on it. Then I put both hands on it and rattled it some more.

The rattles echoed throughout the foyer like chains in a dungeon. I could feel perspiration breaking out between my shoulder blades even though the temperature inside the house was cool. Ghost cool, if you were the type to believe in all that nonsense—which, of course, I wasn't. I knew for sure that my parents' seances were staged. I'd seen my father's finger pushing the glass across the board. I'd pushed the thing myself, to spell out 'this sucks' when my mother had pressured me to join in the last time I visited.

I pulled on the doorknob with one almighty tug and stumbled backwards as it came off in my hands. I regained my balance and stood staring down at the brass ball of the doorknob as if it were a hand grenade.

I tried to put it back where it belonged, but part of the mechanism had come away with the knob. My heart began its frantic flapping up in my throat again. I was trapped inside Alessandro Lucioni's house and night was falling. How on earth was I going to get out? What if he found me skulking around in there? I would look like a complete nutcase. A stalker. A prowler. A first-class idiot.

The windows. *Of course!* I put the doorknob down on the dust-ridden surface of a hall table and went to the nearest windows, which were in a reception/drawing room off the hall. I tried the catches but they looked like they had all been painted over. None of them would budge at all.

I went to the next room along but, while I was able to get one catch undone, the sash of the window must have been broken because it wouldn't lift up. I let out a very rude word—and turned around to see a tall, silent figure framed in the doorway. This time my heart almost leapt out of my throat and bounced along the floor. Then I realised it was Alessandro, and not some ghostly spectre from the past.

But then, he *was* a spectre from the past.

'You scared the freaking hell out of me!' I said.

He cocked an eyebrow in a wry manner. 'Same.'

Quite frankly, I was annoyed he wasn't showing any of the fear or shock he'd alleged I'd caused him. My heart was still hammering so fast I could feel it in my fingertips, and my stomach was like a butter churn set on too fast a speed.

When I'm cornered I always go on the offensive. 'What sort of place *is* this?' I said. 'It's not safe for an adult, let alone a child. You should have hazard signs up, with skulls and crossbones on them. How on earth are you going to have this house ready in a *month*? Have you got rocks in your head?'

He moved further into the room. It was a large room. A very large room. But when he entered it felt like we were in a dolls' house. Or maybe even a matchbox. He came to stand in front of me. I resisted the urge to back away. There wasn't anywhere to go other than through the window that had stubbornly refused to provide me with an escape route.

The closer he got the more my heart raced. *Boom. Boom. Boom.* It was not just pounding in my fingertips but between my legs as well. I could feel the memory of him pulsing through me, heating me inside out. My flesh was hungry, starved, just about gagging for his touch. I could feel its restiveness against the covering of my clothes, as if my body couldn't wait to get naked and feel his wickedly clever hands gliding over every inch of it.

His eyes were dark and inscrutable as they held mine. 'Why are you sneaking around my house?'

I gave him an affronted look. 'I wasn't sneaking. I called on you but no one answered the door.'

'So you let yourself in?'

The way he said it made it sound like I'd committed a crime. But then, breaking and entering was—and I was guilty on both counts. I'd entered his house and I'd broken his door.

'I was just taking a look around,' I said, quickly thinking on my feet. 'I was checking to see if the place was suitable. We at Emily Sudgrove often do home visits.'

One of his dark brows went up again. 'Unannounced?'

'Well, yes, of course,' I said. 'We like to make sure our girls come from good homes. *Safe* homes.' I emphasised the word 'safe'.

Something in his gaze hardened to onyx. 'I can assure you my niece's safety is my primary concern, Miss Clark.'

It was kind of weird, having him call me Miss Clark—even though I'd been the one to insist on it. It was like we were each playing a role in a play. And right now it was feeling more and more like a melodrama. He was looking all stern and irritated, as if he wanted to remove me bodily from the premises, and I felt like a petty thief caught red-handed.

But I could also feel something else pulsing between us. Not just hostility, because that was coming mostly from me. I'm no mind-reader, but I got a sense that he was brooding over something that had nothing to do with our history. There was a wall around him—an invisible fortress that made him appear untouchable. It was like he was weighed down with something. It was in the way he held himself: the braced posture, the rigid set of his jaw, the guardedness about his expression and the shadows that came and went at the back of his eyes.

Was it concern about his sister and his niece? It was an enormous responsibility to be appointed *in loco parentis*. He was used to being a playboy, free to live his life without having to answer to anyone.

He walked back to the door of the drawing room and held it open in a pointed manner. 'I have things to do. I trust you'll make your own way out?'

I gave him a sheepish look. 'Actually, I had a bit of a problem with your front door.'

A muscle ticked near the corner of his mouth. I wasn't sure if it was anger or amusement. It was hard to tell from his expression.

'Oh?'

'Yes, it sort of broke. That's how I got locked in. That's why I was in here, trying to get out of the window.'

It was definitely amusement, I decided. I could see the corners of his mouth twitching and a gleam had come into his darker-than-night eyes.

'There *is* a back entrance.'

Now, why didn't I think of that? I wondered. 'Oh, right…well. Maybe I'll go out that way.'

I made to go past him in the doorway but he put out his arm like a railway-crossing barrier.

'When Beauty trespasses on the Beast's property there's a forfeit to pay,' he said.

I wasn't sure what version of *Beauty and the Beast* he was working from, but it certainly wasn't the same as mine. I looked at the strongly corded muscles of his arm, blocking my escape. He was wearing a light grey cotton T-shirt that clung to his chest and shoulders like cling film. Every sculpted muscle was showcased to perfection—especially his pectorals and biceps. *Oh, dear God, his biceps.*

He had patches of perspiration on his chest and beneath his armpits, and his arms were dusty—as if he had been working on the house. How could someone look so good when they were so hot and sweaty? My insides did a little shuffling thing at the thought of those arms pinning me to a bed while he had his wicked, wonderfully heart-stopping way with me.

I made the mistake of lifting my gaze to his mouth. He hadn't shaved since that morning and his stubble was rich and plentiful, reminding me of the way it had felt scraping along my skin in the past.

I had to curl my fingers into tight balls to stop myself from touching him. I surreptitiously breathed in the scent of him—that beguiling mix of citrus and hard-working male that was as intoxicating as a drug. Not that I've ever *done* drugs. I leave that sort of stuff to my parents.

I curled my fists even harder. So hard I could feel my nails digging into my palms—which is really saying something, as I don't have any nails to speak of. I've been a nail-biter since… Well, since way back.

The urge to touch him was overwhelming. It was like my body was set on automatic. It wanted to do all the things it used to do. Touch him. Stroke him. Kiss him until we were tearing at each other's clothes. My inner core was throbbing with need and he hadn't even touched me.

Alessandro's gaze went to my mouth. I knew that look so well. I hadn't been able to erase that look from my memory even though I had so desperately tried. The smouldering heat of it, the electrifying erotic promise of it, was enough to make my girly bits shiver in rapture.

He lifted his hand and ever so slowly grazed my face with his knuckles. It was such a light touch, barely touching my face at all, but it was as if he had set alive every nerve beneath my skin with an electrode. I felt the pulse of it shoot like a hot wire straight to my core.

'You should've left while you had the chance,' he said, in a voice that sounded like it had been dragged over his gravel driveway before being swirled around in a pot of honey.

I could have pointed out that he hadn't given me the chance to leave, but right then winning an argument wasn't high on my list of priorities. I found myself trans-fixed by his mouth as it came inexorably closer to mine.

My breath hitched and stuttered and then stalled. My heart leapt and then galloped as our breaths mingled in that infinitesimal moment before final touchdown.

My lips all but exploded with fiery sensation as his covered mine. The pressure of his mouth was not too hard nor too soft, but—to borrow from another popular fairy tale—just right. His tongue stroked along the seam of my mouth but he needn't have bothered asking for entry. I was already opening to him with a sound of encouragement that was part whimper, part gasp of delighted surprise.

How could I have forgotten how wonderful his mouth tasted? It was like rediscovering a favourite flavour. My tastebuds tingled and danced and exploded with delight. My tongue met his, darting against it in a come-play-with-me action that made him growl deep at the back of his throat.

He took control of the kiss by spinning me around so my back was against the nearest wall, pinning my hands either side of my head as his mouth supped and sucked on mine. The seductive pressure on my mouth incited me to arch my back and press my pelvis against his in a totally instinctive, utterly primal manner. I wanted to feel his response to me. The swell of his flesh, the arousal that signalled his need for me, which I desperately hoped was as fervent and out of control as mine.

It was.

He was hard and getting harder. I could feel the hardened swell of his erection growing against my body, making me ache with a bone-deep longing. I moved against him wantonly, urging him to take things to the next level. It had been so long since I'd felt desire like this. It was pulsing through me like a force I had no power to control.

There was an element of desperation about his kiss— as if he'd been waiting a long time to feast on my mouth and was making up for lost time. His tongue stabbed and stroked at mine, ramping up my desire until my whole body was trembling with it.

He reached for the tie at the back of my head and my hair fell in a mass of curls around my shoulders. He fisted one of his hands in my hair as he worked his magic on my mouth. The slight tug on the roots of my hair triggered a wave of intense longing deep in my womb.

His mouth moved from mine to blaze a hot, moist pathway down the sensitive skin of my neck. His stubble grazed, his teeth scraped, his tongue salved. I whimpered and melted against him. My legs were like two strands of overcooked fettuccine. I would have slithered to the floor if it hadn't been for him holding me upright.

He moved further down to my décolletage; ruthlessly pulling aside the sensible cotton blouse I was wearing to access the upper curve of my breasts. His tongue licked the valley between before moving up in a fiery blast of heat over each of my curves in turn. He didn't expose my nipples. He didn't have to. They were doing their own little happy dance behind the lace cups of my bra.

His mouth came back to mine as he tugged my blouse out of the waistband of my cotton trousers so he could access my naked skin. I shuddered with delight as his hands glided over my waist and rib cage. His hands were slightly callused, and that added roughness gave his touch a primal, almost dangerous element to it that made my knees feel as weak and wobbly as a newborn foal on ice skates.

His tongue tangled with mine in a heated duel that reminded me of two opponents battling it out for supremacy. I'm not so sure if I was fighting him or myself. My brain had gone into its left-side, right-side dialogue again. The logical side of my brain was saying, *Stop it. Stop it right now.* The other was saying, *Seize the day.*

Alessandro's hands were on my hips now, holding me against his arousal while his lips played with mine in little nips and nibbles and playful nudges.

'Tell the truth, *cara mio*,' he said, in a husky burr that did even more serious damage to the stability of my legs. Possibly permanently. '*This* is what you came here for.'

It was shamefully close enough to the truth for me to push him away with a mocking laugh that unfortunately didn't sound too convincing. 'Nice try, Lucioni, but no. I came here to talk to you.'

He leaned indolently against the door jamb with his arms folded across his broad chest. It was annoying that he showed no sign of our recent lust-fest. I was still trying to tuck my blouse into my trousers and put some order to my hair, but I couldn't find the tie he'd taken out of it. I would have to leave it bouncing around my face like a clown's wig. *Argh!* Why hadn't I made the time to book in for my three-monthly chemical straightening session?

He held something up in his hand. 'Is this what you're looking for?'

I was wary about getting too close to him again. My senses were still screaming in protest because I'd cut short their titillation. Besides, I didn't trust myself. It was galling to think he had such sensual power over me. I didn't let *anyone* have *any* sort of power over me. How could he undo me with one kiss?

My body was still thrumming like a tuning fork struck too hard. The wanting was an ache deep inside, like a hunger only he could satiate. Why had I allowed him to reawaken those wretched needs? It was like being planted in front of an all-you-can-eat smorgasbord after a five-year diet. For years I'd been able to ignore my needs, deaden them, deep-freeze them. But one look, one touch, one potently passionate kiss, and they were active again.

'Throw it to me,' I said.

The corner of his mouth tilted. 'Come and get it.'

I wasn't sure if we were still talking about my hair tie or not. There was a sardonic glint in his eyes that made my stomach free-fall. The air was crackling with the sexual energy of the primal need we had stirred in each other. It was a palpable force that made me hyperaware of every cell of my body, as if my skin had been turned inside out.

I felt it on my lips, where his had pressed and played and plundered. I felt it on my face, where his hand had cupped my cheek. I felt it at the roots of my hair, where his fingers had splayed along my scalp. I could still taste him on my tongue—the hint of mint and good-quality coffee and maleness that was like a potent elixir to me. My breasts were tingling inside my bra, my lady land was contracting, my thighs were quivering, my spine was threatening to unlock vertebra by vertebra.

How could I have walked into this situation so blindly? But maybe I hadn't. Maybe my subconscious had known all along that something like this would happen once Alessandro and I were alone.

'Put it on the table over there,' I said, nodding towards a leather-topped drum table.

He held his hand out with my hair tie right in the middle of his palm. 'You want it? You come and get it.'

That was another thing I could feel pulsing in the air—the collision of two strong wills. We were both driven and competitive people who hated losing. I had already lost considerable ground by responding to him so wantonly. No wonder he was looking so darn smug. He'd crooked his metaphorical little finger and I had come running. But I wasn't going to let him win this. Not on his terms.

Although how I was going to get past him in order to leave was presenting me with a rather perplexing problem.

'Why are you doing this?' I said, clenching my teeth and my fists.

'Doing what?'

I narrowed my eyes to hairpin slits. 'You know what.'

He gave me a guileless smile. 'It's just a hair tie, *tesoro.*'

My lips were pinched so tight I could barely get the words out. 'It's not just about the hair tie, damn it. It's you. You're playing games.'

He tossed the tie in the air and deftly caught it. Once, twice, three times. His eyes were still holding mine. 'You said you came here to talk. So talk.'

I compressed my lips for a moment. The light was fading outside, which made the shadows inside the house all the more menacing. Goose bumps rose and raced along the flesh of my arms.

I crossed my arms over my body and glared at him. 'Why don't you turn on the light?'

'You came all this way to ask me that?'

I gave him a cutting look. 'Don't be a smartass.'

'Right back at you, sweetheart.'

I poked my tongue out at him. Childish, I know, but he had that effect on me.

I knew he was only using those tender endearments to annoy me. I had believed them once. I had really *felt* like his sweetheart. His treasure. His darling. I had loved hearing him say the words. His trace of a Sicilian accent had given them a spine-tingling quality. But they were false—just like his promises of for ever.

My anger blistered inside me, peeling off a layer of my stomach like acid. How could I have been so gullible as to believe he loved me? He hadn't even *told* me. Not in so many words. He had acted like he did. That had been enough for me. I've always been a great believer in actions speaking louder than words. Words are so cheap. Anyone can say *I love you*. It's demonstrating it that's important.

All he had demonstrated was that he was a master at manipulation. He'd charmed me into believing I was the best thing that had ever happened to him. When I'd ended things he hadn't even *acted* being devastated. He'd shrugged it off in an easy-come, easy-go manner that still rankled with me. If he'd felt anything for me—anything at all—wouldn't he have fought for me? Defended himself?

But, no. He'd listened to my spitting tirade and gone all stony-faced and tight-lipped. And why wouldn't he? The woman he'd really wanted had got away. I was just the backup plan. The face-saving fling. What did it matter if I stormed off in a huff? Our four-week fling had achieved what he'd wanted it to achieve. It had showed his ex he'd well and truly moved on.

The trouble was I *hadn't* moved on. I was stuck. My life was on pause. I couldn't go forward because I was too frightened to open myself up to caring about someone enough for them to hurt me. I was watching life from the sidelines. Watching as friends fell in love and got married. Set up homes together. Had babies.

Even my sister was talking about babies. She and Matt were getting married in September, and I was going to be the maid of honour. I was dreading it. It wasn't that I wasn't happy for her. I was. I was thrilled she'd found Matt after that two-timing twat Andy she'd been with before. But it was the thought of everyone asking me if I was seeing anyone. Of everyone looking at me and pitying me for still being single at twenty-nine.

I struck a don't-mess-with-me pose: one hip pushed forward, my arms still crossed over my chest. 'You can't keep me here all night.'

That wickedly sexy gleam was back in his espresso-dark eyes. 'Can't I?'

A frisson of traitorous excitement shot down the length of my spine. 'Holding someone against their will is a crime.'

He moved away from the door and came over to where I was standing. 'Open your hand.'

I didn't care for his commanding tone, but I opened my hand regardless. The sooner I got out of there the better. He placed my hair tie in the middle of my palm and then gently closed my fingers over it, giving my hand a tiny squeeze before releasing it.

'I like your hair loose,' he said.

'I'm thinking of getting it cut off for the wedding.'

His eyebrows snapped together. 'Whose wedding?'

'My sister's.'

'Oh...' Something about the way he said it gave me the impression he was distracted. But then he seemed to gather himself. 'No. Don't do that. Your hair is beautiful.'

I raised my brows at him. 'It's *my* hair. I can do what I damn well like.'

He picked up one of my curls and slowly wound it around his finger. I should have moved away. But apart from the risk of having my hair pulled out by the roots I was having trouble getting my body to respond to the commands from my brain. My body was acting of its own accord, standing close enough to touch him, my hips almost brushing his.

I looked at his mouth and a shudder of longing went through me like the tremor of an earthquake. I knew if he kissed me a second time I might not be able to control myself. I put my hands against his chest, but instead of pushing him back, my fingers curled into the fabric of his T-shirt.

'Don't...' I said in a breathless little whisper that kind of belied my plea.

His mouth hovered just above mine, his eyes hooded in a way that made every feminine cell in my body sit up and beg. His warm breath danced over the surface of my lips, teasing my senses into a mad frenzy.

'Don't what?'

My fingers tightened their grip on his shirt. 'We shouldn't be doing this.' *I shouldn't be doing this. Not again. Never again.*

His lips nudged mine—a playful, teasing little movement that made my lips buzz with sensation. 'You want me so bad you're shaking with it.'

The fact that it was true was just the impetus I needed to get the hell out of there while I still could. Pride came to my rescue.

I gave his chest a hard shove and stepped back from him, flashing him one of my trademark haughty looks. 'I wouldn't sleep with you again if you paid me a million pounds.'

His smile was deliberately—irritatingly—mocking. 'How about two?'

I put my hands on my hips in a combative manner. There's nothing I like more than a fight-to-the-death contest. I was *so* going to win this.

'Make it five and you've got yourself a deal,' I said, privately congratulating myself on calling his bluff. I even did a couple of mental fist pumps in victory.

But then he held out one of his hands, and my stomach fell through the floor as he said, 'Done.'

CHAPTER FOUR

To say I was gobsmacked would be an understatement. I stood gaping at him as if he'd just offered me five million pounds. Hang on a minute. He *had* just offered me five million pounds.

Five million pounds!

My head was spinning. My mouth opened and closed but I couldn't locate my voice. My heart was thumping as if I'd just sprinted up the Empire State Building during an asthma attack. Not that I get asthma or anything, but you get the idea.

'Are you *serious*?' I finally managed to ask— although to be perfectly honest it was more of a squeak.

His gaze was unwavering as it held mine, his expression as enigmatic as ever. 'Don't you think you're worth it?'

I licked my lips. Not in anticipation of all that money, or even the sex—although the thought of having smoking hot jungle sex with him *did* make my pulse skyrocket like crazy—but in panic. I couldn't possibly agree to such an outrageous proposal. *Could I?* The sex I could handle. No-strings sex. No-promises sex. No-plans-for-the-future sex. The fact that money would be exchanged for it made me feel a little uncomfortable...

but, heck, it was a *lot* of money. A truckload of money. Besides, it had been ages since I'd had sex. Years, actually. Why *shouldn't* I indulge in a hot fling with him?

Because he broke your heart the last time, you idiot!

Yes, well, there was that to consider. But five million pounds was nothing to be sneezed at.

I could buy my own Georgian mansion with loads of acreage, instead of living in a tiny flat where I could hear every petty little argument my neighbours had. I could wear ridiculously flashy jewellery and be driven around by a chauffeur in a Bentley or a Rolls-Royce with personalised number plates. I could wear bespoke designer clothes and have a flock of servants to see to my every whim. I could have my very own beautician and nail technician. I could have my hair washed and styled and straightened every day.

My capitalist-hating parents would probably never speak to me again, but still...

I stared at Alessandro's outstretched hand while this inner dialogue ran through my head. With that sort of money I could have anything I wanted...except the thing I *most* wanted.

I brought my gaze back up to his and gave him a tight smile. 'Wow. You nearly had me there.'

'You think I don't mean it?'

I gave a tinny-sounding laugh. 'You must have a very expensive sex-life if you have to dish out that amount of money every time you want to get laid.'

His dark eyes smouldered as they went from my mouth to my gaze and back again. 'I've never had to pay until now.'

I turned away to scrape my hair back into a knot on top of my head, using the hair tie. It gave me something to do with my hands, because I was worried one of them might be tempted to reach out and shake on his deal.

He surely wasn't serious? He was playing with me. Teasing me. Of course he was. I was an idiot to think he would pay five pounds, let alone five million. He was just stringing me along, making me out to be some sort of greedy little gold-digger. The fact that I'd started it by using that old cliché was beside the point.

'You've got the wrong person, Alessandro,' I said, swinging back round with another forced smile. 'Thanks, but no thanks.'

If he was disappointed or annoyed, nothing in his expression showed it. In fact I thought I saw a gleam of respect shining there. 'Would you like a look around the house before you leave?' he asked.

'Sure—why not?' I said, thinking it best to keep casually cool and easygoing in spite of the fact that I might have just rejected—*gulp*—five million pounds.

Alessandro led me out of the reception room into the hall. 'As you can see, there's still a lot of work to be done,' he said. 'There's a lot of structural stuff that has to be sorted before I can get the painters and decorators in.'

'My sister does a bit of home renovating,' I said as I looked around at the paint-stripped hall and bare floors that were in need of a polish and stain. 'She finds it relaxing. But I can't think of anything worse. I guess I'm not so good with my hands.'

His eyes met mine across the distance that separated us. 'I disagree. I seem to remember your hands had very special skills. Skills I haven't come across before or since.'

I turned my face away so he wouldn't see the blush

I could feel creeping all over my cheeks. The same heat was pooling between my thighs. Pulsating need was like a raging fire, racing out of control. I could feel it licking along my flesh with hot, fiery tongues. Why was he so determined to remind me of our past? Surely he realised by now that I was not interested in resuming it.

Although I had to admit I'd been giving him mixed messages. Kissing him the way I had had hardly helped my cause. I'd come across as a wanton desperado. I mentally cringed. How could I have let my guard down like that?

I pushed the toe of my shoe against a bit of broken plaster on the floor. 'Do you really think you'll have this place ready in a month? It looks like it could take six months—maybe even more. It must be costing you a veritable fortune.'

'Money's not an object for me when I have my heart set on something I want.'

His statement had an element of ruthless determination about it that sent another frisson dancing down my spine. I didn't have the courage to look at him. If I looked at him I would cave in and reveal how pathetically weak I was.

I stared fixedly at the peeling paint on the skirting boards instead. 'Clearly not.'

He moved towards another door that led into an east-facing room. 'This is the morning room,' he said. 'It has a nice view over the garden—well, it will once the gardeners get control of the weeding and pruning.'

I looked out of the windows at the garden, where the weeds were almost waist-high. There was a yew hedge surrounding a fountain, but it looked like it hadn't been pruned in years. There were roses in another section, their skeletons spindly and long-armed from lack of winter pruning. There were clusters of bulbs here and there—narcissus and jonquils, and an early daffodil or two offering the only bit of colour and cheer in the neglected landscape.

I turned to look at Alessandro. 'Who owned the house before you?'

'An elderly man who had neither family nor funds nor the health to keep things in shape.'

I thought of all the gorgeous properties in and surrounding Bath. With the sort of money he apparently had at his disposal he could have bought any of his choosing. Why choose a house that needed such a lot of work?

'So why this house?' I asked, voicing my thoughts out loud.

He turned from looking out of the window, his eyes meeting mine. 'It was where my mother grew up as a child.'

I blinked at him in stunned surprise. My mother would be doing cartwheels at this. She would say there was some supernatural force at work that had led me to work and live in Bath because it was where Alessandro's mother had lived as a child. I must admit it was a little freaky, even for a hardened sceptic like me.

'This was her home?'

'My grandparents', actually,' he said. 'She was supposed to inherit it on their death.'

Something about his tone alerted me to an undercurrent of bitterness. His jaw had a locked look about it, as if he were grinding his molars together.

'So what happened?' I said.

A diamond-hard look came into his eyes. 'She got swindled out of it by my father.'

I frowned. 'How did that happen?'

His mouth had an embittered set to it. 'When my grandparents died soon after each other, from cancer and a heart attack, my father tricked her into signing the house over to him. As soon as she signed he divorced her.'

I gasped in disgust. 'That's *despicable*.'

'Yes…he's a class act, is my father.'

'So he's still alive?'

'Not to me.'

The implacable way in which he said the words and the black look on his face made a shiver pass over the back of my neck. 'You really hate him,' I said, rather unnecessarily.

His coal-black eyes pulsated with it. 'Six months after the divorce my mother had a fatal car accident. After the funeral Bianca and I went to live with our father and his new wife.'

'How old were you?'

'Ten. Bianca was seven.'

I pictured him as a ten-year-old boy. Devastated by the divorce of his parents, shattered by the loss of his mother, traumatised by being forced to live with a parent he no longer respected and a new stepmother who might well have resented having to care for two children who weren't her own.

I could see why he hadn't wanted to tell me about his background. It was probably too painful even to think about, much less talk about. And now he had the worry of his sister's health and the responsibility of caring for his little niece.

'I'm really sorry,' I said. 'It must've been a terrible time for you and your sister.'

He moved to the door. 'Come on. I'll show you the kitchen.'

I tried a couple more times to draw him out about his past as we went through each of the rooms, but it seemed the subject was now well and truly closed. He showed me the rest of the house in much the same way as I'd shown him around the school. In a bored tour-guide manner that made me feel I was being a nuisance to him.

Under any other circumstances I would have been angry with him, but after finding out about his bleak childhood it made my emotions towards him somewhat confusing, to say the least. For so long I'd blistered and bubbled with bitterness towards him. My anger had become such an entrenched part of my personality I wasn't sure how to live without it. It was my armour. Stepping out of it would be like being naked in public.

But wasn't his reluctance to dredge over the past more than a little like mine? I was the high priestess of avoidance. How could I blame him for not telling me about *his* childhood when I hadn't told him what had happened in mine?

Once the tour was over Alessandro accompanied me out to my car. He held the door open for me.

'Thanks for showing me around,' I said. 'It's a really nice house. It has loads of potential. I can see why you want to get it back in the family.'

'It's what my mother would've wanted. To see her grandchild enjoy the place as much as she did.'

I put my hand on the top of the car door and then half turned to look at him. In the heat of the moment

I'd forgotten my whole purpose for being there. 'How long has Claudia had her stutter?'

'I'm not sure.'

I raised my brows. 'You haven't asked her mother?'

His expression tightened. 'My sister isn't well enough to handle much conversation right now.'

'She must be very ill.'

'She is.'

I rolled my lips together for a moment. 'Look, I think I can help with Claudia's speech. I've done a special course on language and learning problems.'

I wondered if I should tell him about my own experience. But just as swiftly decided against it. I wasn't going to be fooled into being too open with him. I would treat him like any other parent or guardian at my school. Which meant I would have to erase that kiss out of my memory as soon as possible.

I was about to slip in behind the wheel when his hand came down on mine, where it was resting on the top of the car door.

'Thank you for what you're doing for my niece,' he said.

I glanced at his tanned hand, covering my paler one. A traitorous pulse of longing passed like a current through my body. It was as if he had direct access to my core by that simple touch. It had always been that way between us. I'd felt it the first time he'd touched me outside that café in Paris. I had no immunity from him. For all these years I'd kidded myself I was over him. But every time he touched me I felt that same jolt of awareness. No one else had the same effect on me. I was beginning to suspect no one else ever would.

I brought my gaze up to his. 'I'm not doing anything I wouldn't do for any other child under my care.'

'I called the boarding house before you came,' he said. 'The house mistress told me you'd dropped in after school to see how Claudia was getting on.'

I dismissed his comment with a shrug. 'I often call in on the boarders—especially the young ones.'

His lips lifted in a little sideways smile. 'I would have done it, you know.'

I frowned in puzzlement. 'Done what?'

'Paid you five million.'

I swallowed thickly. 'I'm sure you're not lacking in available and willing partners.'

He lifted a hand to brush back one of my escaping curls and carefully tucked it back behind my ear. 'No. But none quite like you.'

I couldn't drag my eyes away from his lustrous brown gaze. I moistened my lips with a quick dart of my tongue, my pulse doing one of its mad sprints that made me feel light-headed and a little off-balance.

'This is all types of crazy. You. Me. It's not going to happen.'

He traced a spine-tingling pathway along my jawbone from below my ear to my chin. There was no reason why I couldn't have pulled back from his touch but somehow I didn't. I couldn't. There was something in his caress that was almost wistful. Nostalgic.

'Have you been back to Paris since?' he asked.

'No.'

His mouth took on a rueful twist. 'Have I ruined it for you?'

I made a scoffing noise. 'Of course not.'

His eyes searched mine. 'Sure?'

'Absolutely,' I said. 'I was over you as soon as I boarded the plane back home.'

It's a pretty handy skill to be good at lying. My sister and I are masters at it. We've had to be. Years of trying to pretend we had normal parents gave us an edge in the lying stakes. All those schools we had to fit in to made us experts.

We learned early on how to lie through our teeth and how to control our giveaway body language. No nose-rubbing or face-touching. Always maintaining eye contact. No fidgeting. No looking to the right. I've told some porkies in my time, and no one's caught me out.

But for all that I didn't think Alessandro was buying it. His fingertip skated over the vermilion border of my lower lip, triggering sensations I felt all the way to my core.

'So why no steady relationship since me?' he asked.

'I'm a career girl—that's why.'

'Can't women have it all these days?'

I decided against maintaining eye contact. I'm good at lying, but not *that* good. I looked at his tanned neck instead.

'Why do you keep touching me?'

'I like touching you.'

'It's not appropriate, given our…circumstances.' I was going to say *relationship* but thought better of it.

He put his finger underneath my chin until our gazes met. 'You like it too. I can feel it. It's always been like that between us, hasn't it?'

I wanted to deny it. It was just a matter of saying the words. But my voice refused to work. I could feel myself being drawn into that coal-black gaze until I was all but mesmerised. His thumb brushed over my lower lip, sending a riot of sensations through me.

'How much do I have to pay you to have dinner with me?' he said.

'You don't have to pay me,' I said, suddenly embarrassed at the way I'd handled things.

What did money have to do with what I felt about him? If I wanted to spend the evening with him I would. It didn't have to mean we were resuming our fling. Besides, I wanted to dig a little deeper into his background, find out a little more about his sister. A dinner on neutral ground would be just the ticket.

'That's crazy. Dinner's just dinner. We can split the bill.'

His half smile made something in my stomach slip sideways. 'I'll pick you up at eight tomorrow night.'

Why not tonight? I thought with a little pang of disappointment.

As if he could read my mind, he added, 'I have to go to London to check on a transplant patient.'

'How are you managing your work with all this?' I nodded towards the house.

He gave me a weary-looking smile. 'It's a balancing act—probably no different from what your average working woman does every day.'

'True, but surely you've got help? A nanny organised for the holidays and a housekeeper and so on?'

'Can you recommend anyone?'

'As a nanny?'

He nodded. 'I've interviewed four or five, but I can't seem to find what I'm looking for.'

I gave him a cynical look. 'Yes, well, I expect all

the blonde busty bombshells are signed on at modelling agencies instead.'

His dark eyes glinted. 'Or teaching.'

I pursed my lips. 'Flattery doesn't work with me, Alessandro. You should know that by now.'

His knuckles lightly grazed my cheek again, his eyes still holding mine in a lock that tethered much more than my gaze. It was like he was pulling on my most intimate muscles every time he looked at me. The memory of him inside me—stretching me, pleasuring me, filling me and completing me—consumed my senses. I couldn't escape the feelings he stirred in me. I couldn't run away from them and pretend they didn't exist. They did, and they clamoured for attention like baying hungry hounds.

'You don't see yourself as others see you,' he said. 'You find fault where others find perfection.'

I gave a little snort and pulled out of his hold. 'I have to go. I've got lessons to prepare.'

I slipped behind the wheel and reached for my seat belt and snapped it into place. Alessandro closed the door and stepped back from the car. I put my keys in the ignition and prayed. Yes, you read that correctly. I might not believe in the supernatural, but when it comes to my car my feeling is a little prayer never goes astray.

The engine kicked over without a cough or a splutter. Maybe I'd have to rethink my atheist stance, I thought. But as I drove away my car gave a cacophonous backfire that was as loud as a thunderclap.

I glanced in my rear-view mirror to see Alessandro smiling crookedly. *Damn.*

CHAPTER FIVE

I was on my way to my classroom the next morning when my mother phoned. I've told her hundreds of times never to call me during school hours, but she has no concept of the nine-to-five working day. I normally switch my phone off or to silent the moment I get to school, but my mother has this uncanny ability to call me just as I reach for the 'off' button. It's as if she knows I'm about to go incommunicado so she gets in first.

'Poppet, you won't *believe* the vision I had last night.' That was her opening gambit.

Why my mother continues to call me poppet when I've got a perfectly fine name—if you use Jem, not Jemima, that is—is a mystery to me.

'Mum, I'm at school. I can't talk right now.'

'But it's only seven-thirty in the morning!'

'Yes, well…I have to get the classroom ready and—'

'You have no *balance*,' she said. 'I was only saying to your father the other day, you're going to work yourself into an early grave. People can have heart attacks and strokes in their twenties, you know and you're nearly thirty.'

Thanks for reminding me, I thought. 'I'm fine, Mum, really. Now, I really must go as I—'

'But I have to tell you about my vision,' my mother said. 'You were having wild kinky sex with a man.'

I always try to be logical and rational when my mother shares one of her visions with me—especially any that involve sex. She has a very overactive imagination, and the stuff she imagines wouldn't even be allowed in the *Kama Sutra*.

'That's not a vision,' I said. 'It's a dream. It's just your subconscious making a narrative out of what you've been thinking about during the day. That's basically what dreams are.'

'I wasn't dreaming,' my mother insisted. 'I was having a vision. There's a big difference. I know when I'm receiving a sign from the cosmos. It always happens like that. I get this fizzy feeling that won't go away. Last night I closed my eyes and focused on the images coming to me. I could see him clear as day. He was tall and dark and handsome, with really dark brown eyes.'

I felt a little shiver go over my skin in spite of my sandbags of logic. 'That certainly narrows it down a bit,' I said.

'Not only that,' my mother said, 'he looked like that famous doctor. You know—the one who saved Richard Ravensdale the stage actor? It could have been his twin.'

My sandbags were in a sorry shape, but for all that I persisted. 'There's a perfectly logical explanation for your dream...erm...vision. You've probably read something in a gossip magazine about him at the hairdresser's and the image has stuck in your mind. Plus Bertie's Matt is a doctor, so you've—'

'I haven't been to a hairdresser in years,' my mother said. Which is true.

She has dreadlocks—long ones, with beads woven

in. At least she washes them now. There was a time when my parents were anti-shampoo, because they believed toxic chemicals would give us all cancer. Thankfully Bertie and I got head lice, so we were allowed a few toxic chemicals to sort them out.

I glanced at my watch. 'Mum, I really have to dash. Say hi to Dad and I'll call you soon. 'Bye.'

I ended the call and then spent the next hour or two feeling guilty. I always feel like that over my parents. They frustrate me. I know I should accept people for who they are, but there's a part of me that can't accept my parents' lifestyle. They drive me nuts because they have zero ambition. They just want to sit around and navel-gaze, or meditate, or have sex in weird positions while chanting ridiculous chants. Bertie is much more accepting of them, but then I did a lot to protect her from the worst of it.

The rest of the day passed without drama, but I noticed Claudia was still not speaking. I didn't pressure her, for I knew the stress would make her stutter worse.

I spoke to Jennifer at the boarding house and she told me Claudia had slept well and was not showing any signs of homesickness other than seeming reluctant to speak. We talked about my plan to help Claudia with some drama therapy and I told her I would suggest that Alessandro engage a speech therapist as well. Of course I didn't tell Jennifer I was having dinner with him that night.

The prospect of our 'date' had had me in a state of restlessness all day. Whenever there was a moment when I wasn't fully engaged in teaching the girls—when they were working on their own or something—my mind would drift... I would start thinking of how he would look. Would he wear a suit or dress casually? How would he smell? Of lemons or lime or sandalwood or soap? How would his hand feel in the small of my back as he led me to his car?

I was like a lovesick teenager. Talk about nauseating. I kept telling myself we were just having dinner to discuss Claudia's management. It was perfectly legitimate and aboveboard. It didn't mean I had to take it any further. It wasn't as if I was going to jump into an affair with him after what had happened last time.

But no amount of self-talk could take away my attraction to him. It was as feverish as ever—maybe even worse than five years ago. I only had to think of him and my flesh would tingle all over.

I got home late after a staff meeting ran overtime. Normally I enjoy staff meetings. It's a good chance to chat through any issues that have come up with the pupils or concerns about the curriculum. But this time I was fidgeting like I had a bad case of intestinal worms. Miss Fletcher had glanced at me once or twice from over the top of her bifocals and asked if I was all right. I assured her everything was just fine and concentrated harder on taking down the minutes of the meeting.

Once inside the door of my flat I had just enough time to have a shower and do something with my hair. I rummaged through my wardrobe for something to wear, pointedly ignoring the wedding dress bagged in a silk bag, hanging at the back behind my hiking jacket. I selected the classic little black dress I'd bought in a sale when shopping with Bertie.

I'm not a slave to fashion. Unlike Bertie, who adores bright colours and quirky clothes, I have very little colour in my wardrobe. I stick to the basics: black, white, navy and grey. Boring as hell, but I'm not out to impress anyone.

I had only just finished with the hair straightener when the doorbell rang. My heart lurched as I glanced at my watch. It was only seven-thirty. Alessandro had said eight o'clock. I hadn't even done my make-up. Not that I use a lot at the best of times, but I'd figured a bit of facial armour wouldn't go astray—especially since I'd blushed more in the last twenty-four hours than I had in the last five years.

I put down the straighteners and smoothed my hands down my dress, slipped my feet into a pair of heels. He'd seen me without make-up so what did it matter? He'd seen me without *anything*.

I opened the door and found my parents standing there, with big cheesy grins on their faces.

'Surprise!' they said in unison.

I mentally rolled my eyes. I think I did it in reality as well. My parents love surprises. I hate them. Not my parents. Just surprises. I don't like anything spontaneous. I'm a planner. Surprises do not fit into neat plans.

'What are you doing here?' I said. 'I thought you were on a yoga retreat in Salisbury?'

'We cancelled,' my father said. 'Your mother was worried about you. We thought we'd come and stay for a few days.'

Stay? My brain was like a neon sign, flashing PANIC in big red letters. I was about to say it was totally inconvenient and inappropriate of them to turn up announced when I suddenly realised how tired Dad looked. He would have been driving for hours, because my mother had lost her licence a few months ago for speeding. I know… Talk about irresponsible. She maintains she was driving well under the limit, but because she got into a 'discussion', as she called it, with the traffic cop things got a little testy.

'Aren't you going to ask us in?' Mum said with a beaming smile.

'Oh, right—sure,' I said, and stood stiffly as they both crushed me in bear hugs and smacked noisy kisses on my cheeks.

Mum did a full circle of my sitting room once I'd closed the front door. 'Poppet, the feng shui in here is dreadful.' She gave a little shudder. 'That mirror is facing the wrong way.'

'How can it be facing the wrong way?' I said. 'It won't reflect anything if I turn it around the other way.'

My mother gave me a despairing look. 'It should be on *that* wall. It's bad luck to have it facing that way. All the energy will drain out through the front door.'

This time I did roll my eyes. Twice. 'Look, I'm about to go out, so why don't you guys make yourselves comfortable and—?'

'Out?' My mother's eyes were suddenly as bright as searchlights.

'Yes. I have a parent-teacher meeting.'

'Dressed like that?' my father said.

I frowned. 'What's wrong with the way I'm dressed?'

'Nothing,' he said. 'You look lovely. Like you're going on a date or something.'

'See?' My mother said to my father. 'I told you she's seeing someone. A mother just *knows* these things.'

'I am not seeing anyone,' I said. 'I'm just having dinner with…a friend.'

'Don't worry about us,' my mother said. 'We'll make

ourselves at home. I'll make some kale and quinoa muffins for you. We can chat when you get back.'

I glanced at the clock on the wall. 'Erm…you don't want to go and stretch your legs after being in the car all that time?'

'It's dark outside,' my father said.

'And it's starting to rain,' my mother chipped in.

'Right… Well, then, you guys settle in while I put on some make-up,' I said, and headed back to my room.

My mother followed and stood watching me as I applied a bit of powder and bronzer. I mentally prepared myself for one of her lectures on how using make-up was totally unnecessary and just a ploy for cosmetic companies to make loads of money out of women who felt insecure about their looks. But instead of lecturing me she handed me the bronzer brush like a scrub nurse hands a surgeon a scalpel.

'What's wrong, poppet?' she said after a moment or two. 'You seem so tense. I mean, more tense than normal.'

'I'm fine.' I put down the brush and picked up my mascara. It was almost empty, but I managed to get enough out to coat my lashes from practically invisible blonde to brown.

My mother tilted her head on one side as she took in my outfit. 'You know, black really isn't your colour. It washes you out too much. Have you got anything a little more colourful?'

She made a move towards my wardrobe but I cut her off at the pass. I moved so fast I was like greased lightning.

'Don't,' I said, flattening my back against the wardrobe with my arms outstretched like I was guarding the Crown Jewels.

My mother looked at me oddly for a moment, and then with sparkling intrigue. 'What on earth are you hiding in there?'

I worked hard to keep my expression clear of any of the dread I was feeling. The wedding dress was my skeleton in the closet. A taffeta and tulle skeleton of my hopes and dreams.

'I've...erm...got your birthday present in there. I don't want you to see it.'

My mother screwed up her forehead. 'But it's not my birthday until November.'

'I know, but you know how I like to be super-organised.'

The doorbell sounded and my heart slammed against my breastbone. The choice between my mother rifling through my wardrobe or having my father answer the door to Alessandro was an easy one.

I snatched up my purse and dashed out of my bed-room—but my father was already doing the honours.

'Well, howdy-do,' he said to Alessandro, not just shaking his hand but clasping it between both of his as if Alessandro was the Prodigal Son. Or a big-time prophet. '*So* delighted to meet you. Well, well, well—look at you. A fine specimen of manhood. Mighty fine indeed. Jem hasn't been on a date in *years*—or none that we've known about. I'm Charlie and that's Annabel.'

Thankfully my mother had followed me out of my bedroom and now stood with her hands clasped to each side of her face. 'Oh, my God! It's *him*! It's the man in my vision!'

I wanted the floor to open up and swallow me and

spit me out in some other country. Outer Mongolia, preferably. Outer space would have been even better.

'Pleased to meet you, Mr Clark…Mrs Clark,' Alessandro said, somehow getting his hand out of the grip of my father's and offering it to my mother. 'I'm Alessandro Lucioni.'

'Oh, please call me Annabel,' my mother said. 'We're not married. We don't believe in—'

'Right, let's go,' I said, grabbing Alessandro by the arm and all but marching him out of the house before my mother read his mind, his palm, his aura, or whipped out a set of tarot cards and predicted his future.

'Don't do anything we wouldn't do!' my mother called out in a singsong voice.

'They seem like nice people,' Alessandro said once we were in his car. 'Do they live with you?'

'God, no,' I said barely able to suppress a shudder. 'They've just dropped in to stay for a few days.'

I felt his glance come my way.

'You don't like it when they visit?'

I looked at my hands, gripping my evening purse. My knuckles were bone white. I forced myself to relax my grip but the tension was still in the rest of my body. It was like concrete setting along the column of my neck and spine. I get that way every time my parents land unannounced on my doorstep.

I'm a private person. I like my own space. My own routine and timetable. My parents have no concept of personal boundaries. It's not that I don't love my parents. But I like them in small doses—and preferably on neutral territory.

'I would've liked a heads up first,' I said. 'They don't seem to understand that I have a job that means the world to me. Their life is one big holiday. They flit from place to place like a couple of stoned butterflies. They drive me completely nuts. I'll come home and find my furniture all rearranged because the feng shui isn't right. Or my fridge and pantry will be cleaned out so there's no processed food.'

I suddenly gasped.

'Oh, my God!'

The car slowed as he applied the brakes. 'What's wrong?'

'I forgot to hide the steak.'

He glanced at me quizzically. 'The steak?'

'My parents are vegans,' I said. 'They were veg-etarian before that. My sister and I used to sneak in a steak when they weren't looking. I just bought the most delicious eye fillet. It cost me a fortune and now my mother will throw it in the rubbish.' I groaned and banged my head against the headrest. '*Why* couldn't I have normal parents?'

'You don't get to choose your family—only your friends.' It was a well-used axiom, but the way he said it gave it a level of gravitas.

'Tell me about it.' I swivelled in my seat to look at him. 'Tell me about *your* family.'

His expression got that boxed-up look on it. 'I don't want to ruin your appetite for dinner,' he said. 'How did Claudia go today?'

'She was quiet in class, but she seems to be settling in,' I said.

I explained about the speech therapist we had as a consultant to the school and how we would need his approval to engage her services.

'Fine—do whatever needs to be done,' he said. 'I don't care about the cost.'

'For a kid you hadn't met until a couple of weeks ago, you seem to really care,' I said.

He lifted the shoulder nearest me in an indifferent shrug but it didn't fool me for a second.

'She's an innocent child,' he said. 'She deserves a chance to be the best she can be, no matter what her circumstances. As does any other child.'

I let silence slip past while I studied him covertly. He had a grimly determined look on his face. It etched his features into harsh lines that gave him an intimidating air. I liked the fact he was prepared to do anything to protect and provide for his niece. I didn't want to like anything about him, but how could I not admire him for that? Didn't I have the very same values?

'Claudia is a little behind academically, but that's probably because of her language difficulties,' I said. 'I'm working on a special programme for her. She'll get extra tuition from me, and from Jennifer at the boarding house.'

There was a long silence as the car's tyres swished over the rain-lashed roads.

'My sister has a drug problem,' Alessandro said heavily. 'She's had it since she was sixteen.'

'I'm so sorry.'

He flicked me a bleak look. 'I blame myself for not doing more to protect her.'

I frowned. 'But how can it be your fault? You're not her parent. You're her brother. Besides, sometimes teenagers do stuff regardless of the parenting they've received.'

He let out a jagged-sounding sigh. 'I spent most of

my life resenting her. My father spoilt her. She could have anything and do anything she wanted. There were no boundaries.'

'Wasn't he like that with you?'

He gave a scornful laugh that had a sharp edge of bitterness to it. 'No.'

There was a lot of information in that one word, I thought. Not just the way he said it, as if spitting out something vile-tasting, but also the way his body was set. His hands were gripping the steering wheel so tightly I could see each of the tendons bulging on the backs of his hands. And there was a storm of suppressed anger in his gaze as it fixed on the road ahead.

I had an unbearable urge to reach out and touch him. To soothe the pain he was obviously feeling. It was unlike me to be so sympathetic—especially to someone who had hurt me so badly. I would have to watch myself. I wasn't as armoured up as I wanted to be.

I shifted in my seat and held my purse a little tighter. 'What was he like with you?' I asked.

'Tough.' The tendons on his hands now looked like they were going to burst out of his skin. 'Demanding. Strict.' He paused for a beat. 'Occasionally violent.'

I swallowed thickly. 'That's awful… It must've been so hard, having to live with him after your mother died.'

There was another swishing silence. I watched the windscreen wipers go back and forth like twin metronome arms. I couldn't stop thinking about his childhood. How had he coped with his mother's death? How had his sister coped? What responsibilities had Alessandro taken on that made him feel so guilty for his sister's problems? How difficult must it have been to live with the man who had exploited his mother? Was that why he hadn't told me anything of his childhood? Because it had been too bleak and lonely and Dickensian to verbalise?

'He hated me for defending my mother,' he said finally. 'He believed a son should stick with his father, no matter what. He was of the opinion that women were inferior. That they only existed to service the needs of men.'

'Yes, well, I've met a few of that type in my time.' I couldn't stop myself from saying it.

His eyes cut to mine. 'I didn't use you, Jem. I know it probably felt like it at the time, but I really wanted things to work out for us.'

I wanted to believe him. Even after all this time, and with all the simmering hurt that weighed me down so much, I still wanted to believe him. The foolish hope that refused to die annoyed the hell out of me. I thought I'd packed that part of myself away and thrown away the key.

'So why didn't you tell me about your ex-fiancée?'

He looked back at the road. 'I wanted to put it behind me. To move on. I hated thinking about how I'd failed to make someone I cared about happy.' He let out a whoosh of a breath. 'But you're right. I should have told you. It's yet another regret I have to live with.'

'How long had you been with her?'

'All through my specialist training—which, looking back, was part of the problem,' he said. 'I was doing a PhD as well as my fellowship. Work and study took up most of my time. I invested in my career, not in our relationship. She got bored.'

I waited a beat before asking, 'Did you love her?'

There was a pause that seemed to go on for ever, but it was probably only a second or two.

'I think what I loved was being in a relationship,' he said. 'Coming from the background I had, I wanted the security of it. Knowing there was someone who wanted the same things in life. Who had the same values. Although on reflection her values were not the same as mine. It was only when I met you that I realised that.'

Did you love me?

The words were balanced on the end of my tongue like a terrified novice diver on the ten-metre springboard. But of course I didn't say them. I sat there staring at my hands and wondering how different my life would have been if I hadn't met him that day in Paris.

I would probably be married to some guy—a fellow teacher, perhaps—and living in the suburbs. I might even have a baby by now. I would have an ordinary life. A predictable, ordinary life that would have been exactly what I'd wanted right up until I met Alessandro. But meeting him had changed everything. It had changed me.

He had changed me.

He suddenly reached across the console and picked up my right hand. He brought it to his chest, holding it against the deep, steady throb of his heart.

'There were so many times I wanted to call you. To apologise for how I handled things.'

I should have pulled my hand away, but something about the solid warmth of his chest and the husky honey depth of his voice stopped me. It occurred to me then that we had communicated more about our backgrounds in the last few minutes than we had in the whole month we'd been together. It was like we'd been pretending to be other people back then—happy, carefree people who didn't have difficult relatives or issues from the past.

'Why didn't you?' I said, but strangely not in the accusatory tone I'd intended to use.

His hand squeezed mine and I swear I felt the contraction as if his long, strong fingers had surrounded my heart.

'The usual reasons,' he said. 'Pride. Stubbornness. Regret that I'd screwed up yet another relationship so why bother trying to salvage it. Stupid reasons.'

What was he saying? That he had loved me after all?

I could feel my resolve slipping like a silk wrap sliding off a bare shoulder. But then I pulled myself up short. So what if we were communicating now? As far as I was concerned it was too little, too late. I wasn't handing out second chances. No way.

'Careful, Alessandro,' I said, with a return to my mother tongue: sarcasm. 'You might fool me into thinking you were really in love with me back then.'

There was another beat or two of telling silence. A pulsing, simmering silence that made the air tighten.

'Why haven't you had a date in years?' he asked.

I decided I was going to kill my father when I got home. I had it all planned. I would force-feed him my steak. I'd pump him full of chocolate and ice cream and frozen yoghurt. I would stuff a loaf of white bread down his throat. I would tie my mother up and make her watch. It would be death by a thousand processed calories.

'I told you the other day. I'm a career girl. I don't have time for a full-time relationship.'

'What about a fling? Had any of those?'

'Not recently—but, hey, if a guy comes along and

offers me five million quid to open my legs I'll do it. No problem.'

He threw me a hardened glance. 'Don't play the cheap hooker with me, Jem.'

I raised my brows in an exaggerated fashion. 'Cheap? At five million? You could get a blow job around here for two hundred pounds.'

'And you know that *how*?' he asked, with a distinct curl of his lip.

I wasn't sure what demon was riding on my back, but I wanted to push Alessandro into expressing some of the anger I could feel brooding in him. Or maybe it was my own anger I wanted to unleash. God knew I had enough of it.

How *dared* he tell me he had regrets over the way he'd handled things? I'd spent the last five years trying to forget him. How dared he waltz back into my life and apologise? To *communicate*, for pity's sake? It was too late.

'I've slept with men for money,' I said. 'Isn't that what a girl does when a guy pays for dinner?'

His jaw locked so tightly I heard his molars grind together. 'I know what you're doing.'

I glided a fingertip from the top of his shoulder down to his thigh. 'What *am* I doing, big guy?' I said in a smoky whisper.

He sucked in air through his nostrils. 'Stop it. I'm driving.'

'What if I don't want to stop?' I sent my fingertip closer to the swollen heat of him, tracing over the tented fabric of his trousers.

To tell you the truth I was a little shocked at myself, but I couldn't seem to stop my wanton come-and-get-me behaviour. I was relishing in the rush of power it gave me. So far he had been the one with all the power. Now it was my turn to show him he had more than met his match.

He let out a muttered curse and turned the car into a side street so quickly I was thrown back against the seat.

But I wasn't there for long.

The engine hadn't even died when Alessandro's strong arms pulled me towards him and his mouth came crashing down on mine.

CHAPTER SIX

HIS MOUTH TASTED of mint and anger and lust and long-ing. The same intense longing I could feel throbbing through my own veins. His lips moved over mine with devastating expertise, demanding I open to him with a bold stab of his tongue.

I had recklessly taunted the tiger and now I was ex-periencing the full force of his reaction. And, quite frankly, I was loving every pulse-racing second of it.

I received him with a sound of approval that came from somewhere deep inside me. I wound my arms around his neck, fisting my hands into the thickness of his hair, and kissed him back with all the pent-up pas-sion that had been lying in hibernation for what seemed like most of my life.

His freshly shaved jaw scraped the skin of my face as he changed position to deepen the kiss. His arms relaxed their iron grip on me and moved to cup one of my breasts in a caressing and yet possessive movement that made my insides twist and contort with lust. His other hand went to the nape of my neck, underneath my hair. He knew instinctively that it was one of my most sensitive erogenous zones. As his fingers moved in amongst those finer hairs, I tingled all over and my toes curled in my shoes.

His mouth softened against mine, his kiss less punishing now, but no less passionate. Our tongues danced around each other in a cat-and-mouse caper, stopping to play every now and again before doing another round. I heard myself whimper as his lips nipped at mine in playful little nudges and bites that made every cell in my body shudder with delight. His warm breath mingled with mine, his taste lingering in my mouth like the bouquet of a top-shelf wine.

I wanted more. I wanted to get drunk on his kiss. To be completely and utterly intoxicated with him.

He slowly pulled back from me, but my lips clung to his as if they didn't want to let him go. He cradled my face in his hands—a gesture that was sure to win any girl's heart, in my opinion. I looked into molasses-dark eyes that were glittering with hot-blooded desire and felt another fissure open like a fault line in the cold, hard armour around my heart.

His thumbs stroked over my cheeks in slow motion, back and forth in a mesmerising caress that made it impossible for me to think of anything witty or pithy to say. I was in a sensual stupor. Stoned on the power and potency of his masterful mouth and the combustion of passion it had triggered in me.

There was a pleated frown between his brows. 'That was…' he paused for a moment, as if searching for the right word '…unforgivable.'

Unforgettable, more like, I thought.

I moistened my lips with a quick dart of my tongue. 'It's fine,' I said. 'It was just a kiss. No big deal.'

One of his hands cupped my cheek as if it were a

priceless piece of porcelain. His touch was so gentle it made the tight knot of my bitterness towards him un-furl like satin ribbon spilling away from its spool. The pad of his thumb pressed ever so lightly against my lower lip. The desire to suck his thumb into my mouth was almost unbearable. His eyes met mine and I felt a jolt of something hot and electric run through me from head to foot and back again.

'I'm sorry,' he said.

'For...?' I could barely get my voice to work, let alone sound normal. It came out husky and breathy. So *not* like matter-of-fact me.

He drew in a deep breath and let it out on a sigh, his hand still cradling my cheek. 'I don't want it to be like this between us,' he said. 'Fighting. Scoring points. Being bitter.'

I moistened my lips again. 'So...what are you say-ing?'

His eyes went to my mouth, as if he found it the most fascinating thing in the world. And I must admit I found his pretty fascinating—especially when I could see a trace of my lip gloss on his lower lip.

I lifted my hand and blotted it away. 'Buy your own lip gloss,' I said, with an attempt to lighten things.

I was feeling threatened by his disarming gentle-ness. It was reminding me of how easily I had fallen in love with him in the past. It was his gentle sensuality that had bewitched me. He wasn't a man to lose control of his emotions or his passions. He had always been in control. He had shown me that in so many ways. It had built my confidence, made me feel secure and safe and able to express my own sensuality without fear of ex-ploitation. He hadn't steamrollered me or pressured me.

And yet he was a deeply passionate man. I could feel the heat of that simmering passion in his body, sitting so close to mine. I could see it in his gaze when it meshed with mine. I was left in no doubt of his desire for me. I suspected he was in no doubt of mine for him, in spite of all of my paltry attempts to disguise it.

His smile was canted to one side. 'Is it so impossible for us to be friends?' '

I cocked my head in a guarded manner. 'What sort of friends?'

His eyes measured mine for a long moment. The back and forth movement of his gaze to each of my eyes in turn made me feel as if he was seeing beyond the starchy, don't-mess-with-me facade I'd erected over the last few years. I got the feeling he was looking for the girl he'd met in Paris.

But I was no longer that girl...or was I?

Was there a faint trace of the old-fashioned romantic in me? Like an old sweater I should have thrown out long ago but had kept just because...just because it was warm and comforting and stirred a lot of memories.

Why else was I finding it so impossible to resist Alessandro's touch? He had come back into my life and turned it upside down. I couldn't control my response to him. It was programmed in my DNA to respond to him on a primal level. I wanted him—no matter how much he had hurt me. I wanted him regardless. I wanted to feel the passion only he evoked in me. I wanted to experience the rapture of being desired by a man who could have anyone he wanted but for some reason had chosen me.

Wasn't that the thing I found most thrilling? Alessandro Lucioni wanted *me*. I was an ordinary girl and he was an extraordinary man—a gifted man who had saved so many lives, changed numerous lives for the better. He was a leader in his field—a giant on whose shoulders others would one day stand. How could I not be flattered that he wanted me? How could I possibly resist the longing he triggered in me?

I wanted to feel alive again. To feel passion and excitement and the hot rush of lust and release race through my body until I was boneless and mindless and breathless.

'The sort of friends who can put the mistakes of the past aside and move forward,' he said.

'Forward into what?'

My voice was back to normal now. Shoot-from-the-hip normal. Don't-mess-with-me normal. Even though I wanted him, I wasn't going to spring into anything serious. Why would I set myself up for heartbreak and disappointment again? I know how to take care of myself these days. I can separate my emotions from my physical needs. Sure I can. No problem. Men do it all the time. Sex is just sex. It's like eating or drinking. You do it when you're hungry or thirsty.

Sex was just another appetite and I could satisfy it— *temporarily*—with him.

A one-off binge—that was what it would be. A gourmet feast of the senses that would hopefully overload my system so the craving stopped. That's how I cured my chocolate addiction. I ate two family-size blocks and was so sick afterwards I was frothing chocolate at the mouth like one of those chocolate fountains you see at a party.

The reason I ate those two blocks was that I'd seen Alessandro walk into the restaurant where Bertie and

I were having lunch that day. I'm not normally a comfort eater, but seeing him with that blonde had been like a rusty dagger to my heart. They had looked so good together. Like they'd stepped straight out of the pages of a glossy magazine. I could scrub up pretty well if I worked at it, but there was no way on earth I could compete with the sort of glamorous arm candy he squired around. Or employed. Or whatever the case might be.

Reading Alessandro's expression was like trying to read a closed book. I knew there was a lot going on between the covers of his mind, but he was showing none of it on his face.

'Would you be interested in taking it a day at a time to see how things go?' he said.

I screwed my mouth up and shifted my lips from side to side in a musing manner. I didn't want to look too keen. I wanted to appear cool and in control, even though my body was already leaping with excitement.

'What about the school's "no fraternising with the parents" clause?' I said, even though none existed and I was pretty sure he knew it.

He would have done his research. He was that sort of person. He would make it his business to find out everything he could in order to get what he wanted.

His smile was sexily lopsided again. 'Rules can be bent a little to accommodate specific needs, *n'est-ce pas*?'

I wish he wouldn't do that. Speak in French, I mean. How was I supposed to act cool and composed when he made my spine go all squishy and tingly? His voice was not the only thing that undid me. It was that look in his eyes that made my body vibrate with longing. The look that said, *I want you. Now.*

I forced myself to sit primly. My mouth was set in a pursed fashion. My hands were clasped in my lap to stop them from wandering over to where I could see the tenting of his trousers. *Be still, my pulse.*

'You seem pretty confident I'll say yes,' I said.

He picked up a stray wisp of my hair and gently tucked it behind my ear. That and the face-cupping and the speaking French were enough to make any hard-case cynic melt, let me tell you. Every muscle in my body felt like it had turned into a blob of hair mousse.

His eyes went to my mouth in that hooded manner that communicated much more than words could ever do. It was the body language of sex and he was totally fluent.

'It would be a shame to ignore what's still there between us,' he said.

The only thing between us right then was the car's middle console and the gearshift, but I didn't point that out. I knew exactly what he was referring to. I could feel it. I'd felt it the first time we met and every time I'd come in contact with him since. The air changed. The atmosphere became charged. *I* became charged.

My blood pounded through my veins as if I had been injected with a potent drug. I could feel my heart beating against my rib cage like a sparrow trapped in someone's hand. My skin tightened all over my body, as if the bones of my skeleton were pushing outwards so I could get closer to him. My breasts ached for the stroke of his hands, for the rasp of his tongue, for the suck and pull of his mouth. I looked at his mouth and felt another wave of need ricochet through me.

'Here's the thing,' I said, forcing my gaze back to

his. 'I don't hand out second chances. It's another rule I like to adhere to.'

His eyes stayed locked on mine. 'I'm not offering you the same relationship as before, so strictly speaking your rule doesn't apply.'

He was good at the countermoves, I had to admit. But what exactly *was* he offering? And why was I even considering it? Although, come to think of it, maybe that wasn't so hard to answer.

'How would it be different from what we had before?' I asked.

'It would be temporary.'

I'm not sure why those four words should have hurt but they did. *Wham.* It was like a knockout punch to the solar plexus. Not that I showed it on my face or anything. I was Too Cool For School. No pun intended.

'A fling, then.' I stated it without emotion. Like a robot processing data.

He shifted his gaze and stared out at the rain-lashed street with a frown pulling at his brow. 'It's all I can offer now.'

I wiped my hand across my brow. 'Phew! That's a relief. So I won't have to worry about you suddenly springing a romantic proposal on me that I'll have to refuse on principle.'

His gaze cut back to mine. 'Marriage is out of the question.'

I lifted one of my eyebrows. 'That's quite some turn-around from the guy who once couldn't wait to get hitched and make babies.'

His jaw worked for a moment and his gaze swung back to the road. His hands gripped the steering wheel for a beat or two before he leaned forward to restart the engine.

'We'd better get a move on,' he said. 'If we don't show up on time we might lose our booking at the restaurant.'

I sat back in my seat—actually I was thrown back by the g-force of his car—and remained silent for the rest of the journey.

The restaurant was not far from the Roman Baths, and it had more stars than the Milky Way—or so it appeared to me. Even after all this time I still get a little starstruck when I go to posh restaurants. It's because Bertie and I didn't eat out when we were kids. Our parents wouldn't allow it. We weren't taken to fast-food restaurants, let alone fine dining ones.

I was seventeen and Bertie sixteen when we went to our first proper restaurant. Our parents were away on a rebirthing retreat, and thankfully we were left at home. Personally, I could think of nothing worse than returning to my mother's birth canal, as apparently I'd come out upside down and back to front and caused quite a bit of damage on the way through. A fact she likes to remind me of from time to time.

Anyway, Bertie and I rocked up to a mid-priced restaurant—we didn't want to look foolish using the wrong cutlery or something—and we both ordered big juicy steaks. It's kind of a sisterly tradition between us now. Of course we don't tell our parents what we get up to… although if my mother opens my fridge at home I guess the game will be well and truly up.

The *maître d'* showed Alessandro and me to our table as if we were the guests of honour. I suddenly felt self-conscious. Were all the other diners looking at me and wondering what I was doing with Alessandro? Wondering how a plain and ordinary, conservatively dressed primary schoolteacher could possibly interest a man as clever and sophisticated as him? Then I had another thought. Were there any parents from school in the restaurant? I did a quick covert sweep of the room, but thankfully didn't recognise anyone.

We sat down and the waiter took our drinks order. I'm not a big drinker. I'm too much of a control freak. I like to be fully in charge of my faculties at all times and in all places. There's nothing quite like a drink spike when you're thirteen to teach you *that* lesson once and for all.

Alessandro wasn't a big drinker either. At least that hadn't changed, even if his views on marriage and kids had. He had a glass of mineral water while I had a glass of cola. I know it's bad for you. Twenty-two teaspoons of sugar and all that. But if I have the diet variety then there's all those ghastly chemicals to think about. The way I see it, I can't win.

Mind you, I'm lucky it doesn't come back to bite me on the bottom. I'm happy to say my bottom is exactly the same size it has been since I was eighteen. Bertie hates me for it. I can eat and drink pretty much what I want.

I reckon it's the nervous energy that burns all the calories off. I look like I've got it all sorted on the surface, but underneath my ice-maiden mask I'm a basket case. I ruminate. I fret. I chew my nails and pick at my cuticles when no one is looking. I would thumb-suck if I could get away with it. I've been known to roll into the foetal position and rock, but not for a while. Months, actually.

Alessandro looked up from perusing the gourmet menu. 'What do you fancy?'

You, I wanted to say.

I dipped my head and made a show of examining my menu like it was a newly discovered addition to the Dead Sea Scrolls. 'Hmm, let me see.' I even tapped my fingertip against my lips. 'Aha! Beef Wellington with scalloped potatoes and green beans.' I closed my menu and sent him a 'that's settled' smile. 'You?'

He was looking at me as if I were the most fascinating thing on the menu. But then I realised I *was* on the menu. We hadn't said it in so many words, but we'd more or less agreed on a fling. *Hadn't we?* Would we race through dinner and go back to his place? We certainly couldn't go back to mine. Not with my parents there. My mother would have her ear to the wall, listening to make sure I was having tantric sex or counting my orgasms or something.

Alessandro reached for my hand across the table, his long tanned fingers closing gently around mine, his eyes holding my gaze in a sensual tether I could feel tugging on me all the way to my core.

'I've thought about you a lot, *ma petite*,' he said.

'Why do you speak French so much?' I said. 'Why not Italian, given your Sicilian heritage?'

I thought I saw something brittle come and go in his gaze before it shifted to watch his thumb stroking the back of my hand in slow rhythmic strokes.

'I haven't been back to Sicily since I left when I was eighteen.'

'Because of your father?'

His gaze met mine once more. 'My life is in England now. This is home.'

I searched his coal-black gaze for a beat or two. Was he distancing himself from his father by becoming more English than Italian? Had his year in Paris been another part of that distancing plan?

'What sort of work does your father do? Or is he retired?' I asked into the brooding silence.

His hand released mine and he picked up his glass and drank a draught of his water before answering. 'He's a property developer.'

'Successful?'

'Very.'

'Was he disappointed you didn't follow him into the business?' I asked.

That hard look came back into his eyes. 'I didn't ask you out to dinner to talk about my father. Let's talk about something else.'

'I'd like to know more about you,' I said. 'I feel like I'm only now starting to get to know you. You kept so much hidden from me in the past.'

His hand reached for mine again and gave it a tiny squeeze. 'Some things are best not talked about.'

Who was I to argue about that? I had my own dirty little secret.

I must have shown something of my conflicted feelings on my face, for Alessandro picked up my hand from where it was resting on the table and brought it to his mouth. He pressed a soft kiss to my bent knuckles, his eyes still holding mine.

'Tell me about you.'

I could feel every muscle in my body shrinking back from the table, like a snail retreating into its shell, but there was only so far I could go with Alessandro's hand anchoring me to him. 'What about me?'

'Tell me why you chose to teach in Bath.'

I flicked the tip of my tongue over my lips. 'I've always liked the area. I love the Regency period and Georgian architecture. I guess this sounds a bit weird, but I felt kind of drawn to the place. I had other options, but I felt compelled to take the job at Emily Sudgrove. Of course my mother would say it was cosmic intervention, or some such nonsense.'

His smile was crooked and heart-stoppingly gorgeous. 'Maybe it was destined that we would meet again, if only for me to apologise for how I handled things.' He stroked the back of my hand again. 'I've missed you, Jem. Really missed you. I've never met anyone else quite like you.'

I felt a sudden contraction in my chest. Had he loved me? Truly loved me? Or was it his pride that had taken the biggest hit? He had lost his ex just weeks before he met me. Would I be fooling myself to think I was somehow special? Had I been The One? He hadn't actually formally asked me to marry him. But he'd hinted he was going to. The talk of making babies and so on had made me believe I was in with a chance.

'I think you're mistaking a holiday fling for something else,' I said.

His eyes meshed with mine. 'Was that what it was for you?'

I carefully screened my features. 'In hindsight, yes, I think it was.' I gave a not very convincing little laugh. 'It was Paris, don't forget. That city's bound to make anyone think they're head over heels in love.'

His gaze was unnervingly steady on mine. 'So you're not interested in marriage and having a family now?'

'God, no.'

I probably shouldn't have answered so quickly and emphatically. Or given a theatrical shudder. I kept my expression composed, but inside I was thinking of babies. Tiny little squirmy pink bodies with ten little fingers and ten little toes. Soft downy heads and fat little bellies and dimples on elbows and knees. Cute button noses and cupid's bow mouths. Little starfish hands reaching out for mine. Little gummy smiles and happy, contented chortles. The sweet, innocent smell of their milky breath.

I'd always wanted at least three or four kids when I was growing up. I liked the idea of being a family. Of having my own tribe. I wanted the security of marriage because my parents' open relationship had always deeply troubled me as a child. I was worried one or both of them would take off with someone else, and Bertie and I would be left. Or, worse, one parent would take Bertie and leave me with the other.

Even though our parents assured us we would always come first, children don't always believe what they're told. They believe what they feel. What they sense. What they fear. What they dread.

Alessandro's thumb moved over the back of my hand again. 'I always thought you'd make a beautiful bride.'

I could feel a prickly heat coming into my cheeks. 'Weddings are such a ridiculous waste of money,' I said. 'It's just a piece of paper. Look at my parents. They've been together for thirty-one years. They're no less married than any other couple who walks down the aisle of a church.'

'True, but don't most girls dream of being a princess for the day?'

I had been one of those girls. I'd planned my wedding day since I was seven years old. I didn't tell Bertie. I didn't tell anyone, in case they thought I was a soppy fool. It was my private fantasy. A flower-filled cathedral. A beautiful gown with an elegant train and a long flowing veil. A bouquet of orange blossom and white peonies and gypsophila. Rose petals being thrown as I came out of the church with my smiling and adoring husband by my side.

I was jolted back to the moment when I realised Alessandro was still waiting for my response to his question. The heat was lingering in my cheeks.

I fanned my face with my hand. 'Is it just me or is it ridiculously hot in here?' I said. 'They should turn the heating down. It's not good for business. That's why fast-food chains have the air-con on cool. It makes people eat more.'

A half smile kicked up one corner of his mouth. 'Let's order, shall we?'

CHAPTER SEVEN

I BLAME IT on the wine. I only had one glass after I gave up on the cola. I suddenly found the cola too sweet—or maybe it was because I wanted to sit opposite Alessandro and appear sophisticated and cool instead of nervous and on edge. He had unsettled me by asking me such probing questions.

So I sipped the wine and because I hadn't had alcohol in ages it went straight to my head... Or should I say straight to my tongue.

Alessandro took one of my hands—the one that wasn't holding my glass to my lips and all but draining it—and asked, 'Why were you so uneasy about sex when we first met?'

I gulped the last mouthful of wine down in an audible swallow—which is really saying something, as there was background music playing: romantic and emotionally stirring ballads that were just as powerful as the wine.

'P-pardon?'

His hand was so gentle against my fingers it was like he was cradling a rare and precious butterfly. As if it was the very last one on earth. His gaze was soft. Supportive. Understanding.

'I know you told me your first time wasn't great, but it was more than that, wasn't it?' he said, and when I didn't say anything he went on, 'I've thought about it a lot over the years. It's haunted me, actually.'

I swallowed again and wished I could have another glass of wine. Brandy, even. A whole bottle. No, make that a whole distillery.

'Don't use that sort of language around my mother,' I said, in an attempt to lighten the atmosphere between us. I didn't want to do deep and serious with him. I had to keep things light and casual. Under my control.

He gave me one of those lopsided smiles that tugged so painfully on my heartstrings. 'You do that a lot,' he said.

'I do what a lot?'

'Use wisecracks and humour to escape intimacy.'

I laughed—which kind of proved his point. But then I blushed, and felt stupid and exposed and more than a little tipsy. I put my wine glass down but misjudged the edge of the table, and it would have fallen to the floor if he hadn't reached out and steadied it with his free hand.

'Jem.'

Maybe it wasn't the wine's fault. It was the way he said my name…the velvet quality to his voice that was like a warm, protective cloak over my scraped raw nerves. I looked at his hand sheltering mine, the long tanned fingers capable of such strength and yet such gentleness. Or maybe it was his melted chocolate gaze… holding mine in that tender way that made me wonder all over again if he had a remnant or two of feeling for me even after all this time.

I felt like I had a wishbone stuck in my throat. I had to swallow a couple more times to clear it. And then it all came tumbling out. Once I started I couldn't stop. It was like I had been waiting years—sixteen years, to be exact—to tell someone what had happened.

'I was living in a commune with my parents when I was thirteen,' I said. 'I hated it. I didn't belong there and neither did my sister.' I took a breath that scored my already tight throat. 'I was worried about Bertie because she always got teased. She didn't know how to stand up for herself. The other kids were feral, but there was this one boy...a bit older than me...who seemed really nice. I felt like I could talk to him, you know? I felt like he understood because his parents were like mine... Although looking back I think they were much worse. They were stoned out of their minds most of the time. They didn't have a clue what their precious son was up to when their backs were turned.'

I looked up at Alessandro's expression and it gave me the courage to continue. I got the feeling if *he* had been at that commune no one would have laid a finger on me.

Not on his watch.

'I was too naive to know I was being manipulated,' I said in a hollow-sounding voice. 'He made me feel safe and comfortable so he could... Well, you can probably guess the rest. He must have slipped something into my glass of orange juice because I woke up to find him...' I blinked a couple of times and swallowed again before I could continue. 'It was over in seconds. Thank God for trigger-happy teenage boys, huh?'

Alessandro's hand gripped mine, as if he was pulling me back from a thousand-metre drop. His expression was full of anger and disgust at what had happened to me, and yet there was compassion for me all at the same time. The muscles on his face twitched. Tensed.

Pulsed. His jaw locked. His mouth flattened. His eyes flashed and then flickered with pain. Flashed again.

'If I knew who he was I would tear him apart with my bare hands,' he said.

I'm not one for violence or revenge or anything, but his words gave me a sense of closure I had never felt before. Or maybe it was because I felt safe. Finally.

'Karma's probably got him by now,' I said. 'He's probably died of a drug overdose or is languishing in prison over some heinous crime.'

'Did you tell anyone?'

I bit my lip until I felt pain. 'I considered it...but who was going to listen? My parents weren't the over-protective sort. They were—still are—into free love. I was terrified they might think I was making too big a deal out of it. That I was too uptight and probably gave out the wrong signals and should get over myself... blah-blah-blah. The usual victim blaming that goes on. I didn't tell Bertie because... Well, she's my little sister and I didn't want her worrying about me.'

His fingers gently stroked my hand. 'So you bottled it all up and put on your tough face?'

I wasn't anywhere near locating my tough face right then. It was like suddenly finding myself naked at a black-tie function. I don't think I've ever felt quite so exposed. And yet oddly enough I didn't feel shame. Not in Alessandro's presence. Not while he was wearing that protective and compassionate expression.

I glanced at my empty wine glass with a rueful look. 'I should never drink alcohol. Or orange juice.'

He brought my hand up to his mouth and ever so gently placed his lips against my bent knuckles, all the while holding my gaze.

'Thank you.'

'For what?'

'For trusting me enough to tell me.'

I screwed up my mouth but for some reason I couldn't find anything funny and diverting to say. I had to swallow again and blink. Rapidly.

'I wish they wouldn't play such soppy music in restaurants.' I gave my eyes a quick swipe with the back of my free hand. 'I bet they do it so the patrons comfort eat.'

He blotted one of the tears I couldn't quite control with the blunt tip of his thumb. 'Do you want to get out of here?'

'Where would we go?' I said. 'My parents are probably working their way through the *Kama Sutra* by now.'

He looked into my eyes. I got the feeling he was seeing behind the humour. Behind the smart-ass wisecracks. It was a strange but pleasant feeling, having someone come that close and not be fooled by the facade.

'How about my place?' he said.

I gave him a speaking look. 'Do you even have electricity at your place?'

He smiled one of his heart-stopping smiles. 'We can make our own.'

It was as we were on the way to his place that the enormity of what I'd done hit me. *I Had Told Someone.* I had told Alessandro—the man I had hated for the last five years. I had unzipped my chest and retracted my ribs and laid my bleeding heart bare.

I had never done that before. Not with anyone. I am not a confidence sharer. I don't even do it with Bertie. Sure, I tell her stuff. We chat like sisters do. But I have never told her of the doubts and fears and anxieties that have plagued me since…that night. Or even before that night.

I'm the strong one in our family. I've had to be. I took on that role at a young age and no one was going to wrench it off me.

Not even some lousy scumbag of a teenage boy who didn't know the meaning of the word *consent*.

But now I had allowed Alessandro to see behind the mask of ice that had served me so well. Global warming had nothing on me. The big melt had set in. I could feel it. I had a warm, mushy feeling right in the centre of my chest. Had I made a mistake in telling him? Would it make him feel sorry for me? Pity me?

I looked down at my hands. One of my cuticles was bleeding and I hadn't even realised I'd been picking at it.

But then Alessandro's left hand reached for my right one and brought it up to his chest, laying it right over the steady beat of his heart. His eyes were still on the road but the deep burr of his voice reverberated through my palm and somehow soothed the pitching-paper-boat-in-a-whirlpool panic in my stomach.

'You're safe with me, *ma petite*.'

I didn't answer. I would have if I'd been able to locate my voice. Instead I sat there wondering how on earth I could have thought I'd hated him for the last five years.

We were almost at his house when my phone rang. I didn't hear it at all, because I'd had it on vibrate for while we were in the restaurant, but Alessandro glanced at my bag and said, 'Aren't you going to answer that?'

'Answer what?'

'Your phone.'

'Gosh, you must have excellent hearing,' I said as I fished it out.

I grimaced as I saw it was my mother. I considered not answering it, but then I thought I might as well tell her I wouldn't be home for another hour or so.

'Hi, Mum. Listen. I've had a change of plan—'

'You have to come home,' my mother said in a strained and panicky voice. 'Your father's not well and I don't know what to do.'

Alessandro must have heard my mother's voice for he asked, 'What are his symptoms?'

'Mum, what are his symptoms?' I relayed his question.

'He's got chest pain and he's sweating and pale.'

'Call an ambulance,' Alessandro said to me. 'Tell her we'll be there in five minutes.'

And then, giving me a reassuring look, he swiftly pulled in and did a U-turn to take us back to my house, not quite speeding but with measured urgency.

The ambulance hadn't yet arrived when we got there. Alessandro took charge in a manner that was both calm and professional, which went a long way to allay my panic—not to mention my mother's. But even so my inner hysteria ran on wildly for a bit.

My father sick? He was *never* sick. I can't remember the last time he was ill, apart from a brief back-pain episode when he picked up Bertie and pulled a muscle or two, which he always reminds her of when he sees her. A bit like my mother and her birth canal. My father was usually robustly, disgustingly healthy. Now he was going to hospital in an ambulance.

My stomach clenched. What if he didn't come out?

My father was in the spare bedroom, lying on the bed. He was dressed as Superman. My mother had put on my bathrobe but I had a feeling that was all she had on. I know. Dead embarrassing. But it could have been much worse. I once came home to find my dad dressed in a dungeon master's costume and my mum in a skimpy leather bikini with a whip in her hand.

To his credit, Alessandro didn't mention what either of them was wearing. He went straight into highly trained specialist mode. He took a history while at the same time measuring my father's pulse and taking his blood pressure, and listening to his heart with the stethoscope he'd produced from the doctor's bag he'd sourced from the boot of his car.

Within a few minutes the ambulance arrived and Alessandro filled in the paramedics with my father's details and directions on what should happen by way of tests when they got to hospital.

'I'll call the hospital to let them know he's coming in under me,' he added.

My mother looked at Alessandro as if *he* were Superman. 'You're going to take care of him?'

'If that's what you'd both like,' Alessandro said. 'Of course I can always refer Mr Clark to someone else if you'd prefer?'

'No!' My mother was emphatic. 'You're the best. Everyone says you are. That's what you want, isn't it, Charlie?'

My father gave a thumbs-up sign, because he was wearing an oxygen mask, and the paramedics wheeled him out to the ambulance.

'Do you want to go with him in the ambulance?' Alessandro asked my mother.

My mother clutched the edges of the bathrobe together. 'I don't want to get in the way.'

'Mum,' I said, taking her arm, 'why don't you get dressed and we'll follow in my car?'

'I'll drive you,' Alessandro said.

My practical nature had thankfully overridden my panic by now. 'But you'll need to stay in London, and I'll have to get back to school in the morning.'

He gave a brisk nod, but then reached for my hand and gave it a gentle squeeze. 'Try not to worry,' he said. 'He'll be leaping from tall buildings in a single bound in no time at all.'

The door was barely closed on his exit when I turned to my mother and hugged her. Yes, I actually hugged her. It's not something I feel comfortable doing, as my mother has a tendency to lean right in and smother me.

'He'll be fine,' I said, hoping it was true. I couldn't imagine my parents without the other. Mum and Dad. They were a team—a weird and wacky team at times, but still a team.

Mum's arms all but cut off my circulation as she wrapped them around me. 'I was so scared,' she said. 'I didn't know what to do. It was so terrifying to see him like that. I thought he was going to die while we were having—'

'Yes, well, that would certainly have been incredibly embarrassing,' I said, somehow managing to extricate myself from my mother's octopus-like hold. 'What were you *thinking*? Dressing up is for kids, not adults.'

'Don't go all preachy on me,' my mother shot back with uncharacteristic heat. 'We weren't doing anything wrong. We often dress up for sex. It makes it more exciting. I didn't even realise he was ill. He never said. He could have died.'

'And how mortifying would *that* have been, with him dressed as bloody Superman?' I said.

My mother pouted. Yes. And a woman of fifty-five pouting is even worse than one wearing a skimpy leather bikini, in my opinion.

'You're just jealous because you're not having sex,' she said. 'You're too uptight to let anyone close enough to touch you. You stand like a shop mannequin when someone hugs you. What's *wrong* with you? Loosen up, for God's sake.'

I clenched my fists. I knew it was unfair of me to rise to her bait. We were both upset by the evening's events and in no frame of mind to talk sensibly and reasonably.

'Yes, well, thanks to you almost giving Dad a heart attack, no one will be touching me tonight,' I said. 'I was going to go back to Alessandro's place and...and... hang out.'

'See?' My mother stabbed her finger at me. 'You can't even say the word "sex". You're so prudish! I sometimes wonder how you can possibly be my daughter.'

My temper was well and truly ignited. I could not pull back from the tirade now the fuse had been lit.

'Yeah, well? Guess what?' I said. 'Sometimes I wish I *wasn't* your daughter. I wish I'd been born into a *normal* family. One where people look out for each other instead of spending their time gazing into their navels or wandering around the country chanting bloody mindless mumbo jumbo while their daughters got bullied or...or...worse.'

I couldn't say the word. The ugly word that described

an ugly act. My experience was mild compared to others. I knew that, and yet it didn't give me the comfort it should.

My mother's face went from attacker mode to bewildered. 'What are you talking about? You had a *lovely* childhood. You were free to explore without the suffocating social structure that shuts down creativity. Look at how well you and Bertie have done. Doesn't that prove our relaxed approach worked?'

'What sort of ridiculous logic is *that*?' I threw back. 'You weren't *there* for us, Mum. Nor was Dad. Not when it counted. Most of the time you let other people do what you should've been doing. Like me, for instance. I was always watching out for Bertie. But no one was watching out for me.'

My mother was still shaking her head in denial. 'No. No. *No*. You sound just like your grandmother when you carry on like that. We wanted you to be independent. To be able to enjoy the magic of childhood without restriction.'

I drew in a breath that felt like it was full of chopped up razor blades. Bitter, angry tears prickled at the backs of my eyes. 'I was raped when I was thirteen years old. Did you hear me, Mum? *Raped*.'

My mother blinked at me as if the lights in the room were suddenly too bright. 'Are you sure?'

Typical, I thought, with a rush of bitterness so powerful I wanted to scream the scream I hadn't been able to scream sixteen years ago out of fear and shame and shock.

'No,' I said with heavy sarcasm. 'I thought I'd just throw that in there. Of *course* I'm freaking sure. Not that you would've noticed. You and Dad were probably too busy swinging with that other couple at that stupid commune.'

There was a cavernous silence.

Then, right in front of me, my mother's face looked like a paper bag that had been crumpled. It completely folded in on itself. She pressed her lips together, but even so, I could see the bottom one had a distinct quiver.

It was a moment or two before she spoke. 'I need to get to the hospital to see your father. I have to get dressed. I have to stop by the ATM and get some money to buy him some pyjamas. He doesn't have any. He always sleeps naked. I have to get his toiletries bag. I have to—'

'I'll do it,' I said, taking her by the arm and leading her to the spare room. It was as if I was now the parent and she was the child. *So what else is new?* I thought. 'You get dressed while I pack his things.'

As I packed my father's belongings I watched my mother out of the corner of my eye. She was like a woman of ninety. She was dithery and her movements as she pulled on her clothes were shaky, as if she couldn't get her fingers to work.

I wished I hadn't told her about the… Well, you know. Maybe that's why I'd never told her. I knew this would happen. She wouldn't be able to cope with it.

As usual, I would have to cope alone.

I left her for a moment while I called Bertie. 'Don't panic, but Dad's just been taken to hospital with some chest pain.'

'Oh, no!' Bertie said. 'Is he all right? Which hospital? Who's he coming in under? Do you want me or Matt to refer him to—?'

'It's all under control,' I said. 'Alessandro is dealing with everything.'

Suddenly I realised how comforting it was to know that. I wouldn't have to be the grown-up with him. I could collapse in a heap and sob like a little kid if I needed to. Not that I would ever do that, but still…

I could practically hear the light bulb going on in my sister's head. 'Alessandro Lucioni is taking care of Dad?' she said. '*The* Dr Lucioni? Cardiac surgeon to the stars?'

'He's just another heart surgeon, Bertie,' I said, in my sensible big-sister voice. 'I bet you have five or six at St Iggy's.'

'None quite of his calibre,' Bertie said. 'How come you got him so quickly? He has a waiting time of months. A year, even.'

Here comes the tricky bit, I thought. 'Yes, well… he happened to be in the area and I was able to call in a favour.'

'I *knew* it!' Bertie said. 'I didn't recognise him at first. I was too busy paying the bill after you shot out of that restaurant the other week. You and Alessandro Lucioni. *Wow*. Double wow. Wait till I tell Matt.'

'Don't get ahead of yourself,' I said. 'We're not seeing each other or anything. His niece is in my class, that's all.'

'That's *all*?'

There used to be a time when I could fob Bertie off with a look or a clipped word or two. But since she's fallen in love and gotten engaged to Matt she's grown some serious backbone. It's kind of scary.

'We'll talk about Alessandro and you some other time,' Bertie said. 'I'll meet you at the hospital. Mum will need some support. So will you. What a horrible fright you must've had, you poor darling. Is that where you both are now?'

'Not quite,' I said. 'Mum couldn't go with Dad in the ambulance. She had to get dressed first.'

I could almost see Bertie rolling her eyes. 'Right. Well, drive safely. And don't worry. Dad is in fabulous hands.'

I for one could more than vouch for that.

CHAPTER EIGHT

MY MOTHER AND I drove to Alessandro's hospital in London in a bruised silence. I opened my mouth a couple of times to apologise for upsetting her but then I stopped. Why should *I* apologise? My timing might be a little off but I'd said what needed to be said. Not that it made me feel any better or anything.

I felt miserable.

Bertie and Matt were there when we arrived, which made it easier for me to blend into the background. They gave my mother a hot drink—not coffee or tea, because my parents were currently off caffeine—and sat with her and explained everything that was going on. Matt and Bertie were both doctors, so this was their territory, and although it wasn't their hospital at least they knew the language.

Bertie is good at the emotional support stuff. She's also an excellent hugger. She gave our mother the sort of hug I wish I knew how to give. And kisses. Lots of them. She even did some hair stroking. Mum soaked it up and gave Bertie a grateful, wobbly little smile that made me feel even more of a cow.

Alessandro came out to the relatives' room where we had gathered. Introductions were made and I watched as

Bertie eyed him as if assessing his suitability as brother-in-law material. I kid you not. My sister is totally obsessed about weddings. She surreptitiously gave Matt a nudge before glancing at me.

I was poker-faced.

'Your dad has a badly leaking mitral valve,' Alessandro was saying. 'Probably as a result of a childhood respiratory infection. He badly needs mitral valve replacement, so we've scheduled surgery for the morning. A valve replacement is normally straightforward these days...'

He stated the risks and benefits but I was barely listening. All I could hear was his doctor-in-control voice. The competent-man-in-charge voice. The knight who had come to the rescue. My very own Superman...

Erm...come to think of it, maybe not Superman.

I looked at Alessandro's hands and imagined where they might be right now on my body if it hadn't been for my father being taken ill.

So much for my poker face. Bertie winked at me and I felt a blush crawl like fire all over my cheeks.

Alessandro spoke to Matt while Bertie leaned in closer to me. 'That's *all*?' she said, in a you-can't-fool-me voice.

I tried my prim and proper look, because it suddenly occurred to me that I needed to talk to her before my mother got there first. 'Look, there's something I need to tell you.'

Bertie led me to another room, further down the hall. 'What?' she said, once we were out of earshot.

Telling Bertie was like telling Alessandro. Once I'd finished I wished I'd done it years ago. Why hadn't I realised before now that she would be strong enough to cope with it? She might be a little scatty at times, and get herself into crazy farcical situations now and again, but she was a warm-hearted, compassionate person who loved me unreservedly.

She hugged me, and for once I didn't stand stiffly like a cardboard cut-out version of myself. I relaxed into the flower-scented warmth of her and might even have let a tear or two escape, but I had it under control once she pulled back to look at me.

'Does Alessandro know?' she said.

'I told him earlier this evening.'

'Wow.'

I frowned. 'What's with all the wows? I told you, there's nothing—'

'Not yet,' she said, brown eyes twinkling.

I hiked a shoulder up and down. 'I might consider a fling with him, just to get him out of my system.'

This time Bertie frowned. 'A fling? Don't you think you're worth more than that?'

'It's all he's offering,' I said. 'And I'm fine with it. I don't want what you want. You know that.'

Bertie put her hands on her hips like she was suddenly the older sister. 'You *do* want it. You just don't want to risk losing your heart a second time.'

I gave her a hardened look. 'I wasn't in love with him then and I'm certainly not now.'

'You are *so* in love with him—otherwise why would you have avoided him all this time?' Bertie said.

I shouldered open the door. I didn't want to discuss the feelings I could feel tiptoeing around the edges of my heart as if they were looking for some sort of entry point. Where was my cynical carapace when I needed it? The crust of my heart had softened like hospital toast. *Urgh*.

'We'd better see what Mum's up to,' I said.

Bertie gave a light, affectionate laugh that twisted my guilt screw another notch. 'God, yes,' she said, and followed me out. 'She's probably rearranging all the bedpans for better feng shui or something.'

'Someone should tell her it's a load of crap,' I quipped.

Alessandro waited until everyone else had left before he spoke to me. He took me to his office on another floor of the hospital. It was a neat and ordered room, with loads of surgical textbooks and his degree certificates set in simple but elegant frames on the walls. If he didn't stop it with the studying he was going to run out of wall space, I thought. How many qualifications did one man need? His desk was made of polished timber, and a computer and a stack of paperwork took up two thirds of it.

'Sorry about the mess,' he said.

'If this is a mess, I'd hate to see you on a tidy day.'

He studied me for a quiet moment. 'You okay?'

I stopped picking at that same hangnail I hadn't even been aware I was torturing and faced him squarely.

'Sure. Fine. Just brilliant. My dad almost had a heart attack having sex while dressed as Superman—which every doctor, intern, resident, registrar, orderly, nurse and cleaner in this hospital now knows—but, hey, all in a day's work, right?'

His expression had that soft and compassionate look about it. 'They're quite a pair, aren't they?'

I rolled my eyes and huddled into myself by wrapping my arms around my body. 'That's not all...' I took a breath and let it out in a whoosh. 'I kind of attacked my mum after you left.'

His brows drew together. 'Attacked in what way?'

'Verbally.'

He gave an understanding nod. 'It happens. Emotions often run high in a crisis.'

I chewed at my lip for a beat or two. 'I told her what happened when I was thirteen. I kind of blamed her and my father for it.'

His frown deepened. 'How did she take it?'

'The way I expected she would—which is why I didn't tell her before.' I started to pace the floor like a parrot on a perch. In a finch's cage. 'Why can't she be like other mothers? Why can't she be normal, for God's sake? Why can't *both* my parents be normal?'

He came over and put his hands on my shoulders from behind me and held me close. The shelter of his tall frame standing at my back was comforting and yet headily arousing. I wanted to turn around and slam myself into him—slake the need that was clamouring inside me. I don't know how I refrained from doing it. Maybe it was the way he was holding me just slightly apart from his body, as if he knew this was not the time and place.

'You're tired and overwrought, *ma chérie*,' he said. 'Come back to my place with me and get some rest.'

I turned to face him. 'But I have school tomorrow.'

He brushed a corkscrew of hair off my face and anchored it behind my ear. 'You could take the day off—or drive down in the morning.'

I bit my lip again. I was sorely tempted, but I kept thinking about little Claudia. She was still so new to the school. I wanted her to be able to rely on me. I was her teacher. I took that responsibility seriously.

'I can't,' I said. 'I might get held up in traffic and then Claudia will panic at having to deal with a fill-in teacher.'

He slid his hand to the nape of my neck and tilted my face up. His eyes had that tender, lustrous quality to them. 'Will you be able to drive home now? It's a two-hour journey at least. Aren't you exhausted?'

'I'm fine,' I said. 'I had three coffees in the waiting room. I'll be awake for the next week. Anyway, it'll be quicker driving at this time of night.'

He slowly brought his head down until his mouth was just above mine. 'Until tomorrow night, then.'

'What are we doing tomorrow night?' I asked.

He smiled against my lips. 'Guess.'

And without waiting for me to answer he kissed me.

I was right about those coffees. I barely closed my eyes all night, even though I had a good run back to Bath in record time. I tossed and turned and fidgeted. I re-lived that kiss a thousand times. The way his mouth had moved against mine—tenderly, in an exploratory way, as if rediscovering a taste for something he had long given up and now craved.

It had been a kiss of promised passion, an anticipa-tory kiss that had made every cell in my body quake with need. His tongue was gentle with mine. Not pushy or too overpowering. I got the feeling he was kissing me as if it were my first kiss. The kiss I should have had as a teenager.

I was drifting into dangerous territory with him. I knew it and yet I couldn't stop myself from dreaming about him… Well, I would have dreamed about him if I'd been able to get to sleep.

I gave up in the end, and got showered and ready for school by six a.m.

Bertie sent me a text, bless her, asking if I was okay. I sent her one assuring her that I was fine. We often communicate using emoticons. But this time I couldn't find one to adequately describe how I was feeling. I felt worried about my father, guilty about my mother, and full of excitement about seeing Alessandro tonight.

There was one other thing I was feeling, but I wasn't going to acknowledge it in case it took a foothold.

There was no way I was going to fall in love with Alessandro.

I wasn't *that* stupid.

After lunch I did a drama lesson with my class. The other children were excited but Claudia hung back, obviously intimidated by the thought of having to act in front of the class. I had it all planned, though. The exercises would be whole-class exercises at first. There would be non-speaking roles to begin with, and then I would up the ante.

It worked like a charm. She was a brilliant little pot plant for the first scene—in fact much better than some of the other more outgoing pupils. She stood with her little thin arms stuck out like branches. And when I said someone had forgotten to water the pot plant she visibly wilted.

I was thrilled.

Then I asked the class to pretend to be puppies that wanted someone standing outside the pet shop to come in and buy them. Claudia was amazing at it. She put on this little take-me-home-with-you face that made me feel like taking her home right then and there.

Then I asked individual pupils to act out certain emotions. I told them to use words or gestures or expressions—whatever they wanted. We did sadness, anger, excitement and happiness. The only one Claudia had trouble with was happiness. Her smile looked a little forced.

I knew the feeling.

Then I moved on to speaking parts. I told the children to work in pairs and I asked Claudia to pretend to be someone who was unhappy with a gift she'd bought from a store. Her partner was to be the unhelpful assistant. What a little champion Claudia was. She morphed into the role as if she had been born for the stage. There was no stuttering. No hesitancy. She put her hands on her hips and stared down the other pupil, insisting on getting a refund. The whole class clapped when she was done.

I can't remember a time when I felt more satisfied as a teacher.

'You're looking pretty pleased with yourself,' Lucy Gatton said when I went into the staffroom at the end of the day.

I told her about Claudia and how well she had performed. 'It was fantastic. I think we should put her in the end-of-term play. We should give her the leading role. It will be brilliant for her. She's a born actor. It's like she totally morphs into the role.'

Lucy cocked her head at me. 'This isn't a case of nepotism, is it?'

I immediately bristled. 'What do you mean?'

She gave me a knowing look. 'You and her uncle?'

I tried to look nonchalant, but right then and there I thought my six and seven-year-olds would have done a much better job. 'There's nothing going on between her uncle and me.'

'Then why were you seen having dinner with him last night?'

I wondered who had seen us. I hadn't noticed anyone—although that didn't mean no one had been there. I'd been more than a little distracted by Alessandro's company. Not to mention having that tongue-loosening glass of wine. Anyone could have seen us and reported it back to the school gossip network.

'We met to discuss Claudia's specific educational issues,' I said, with just the slightest elevation of my chin.

Lucy snorted. 'And what did you do *after* that?'

I pressed my lips together and then blew out a breath. 'Actually, he came back to my place and sorted out a health issue of my father's. He transferred him to London and operated on him this morning.'

Lucy looked a little taken aback. 'Is your father all right?'

'He's fine,' I said. 'Al—Dr Lucioni texted me during break.'

In fact, Alessandro had called me and left a very reassuring voicemail, telling me how much he was looking forward to seeing me tonight, but I didn't want her to know that.

'Everything went well. My father will be out of hospital in a couple of days.'

Lucy was still looking at me as if she wasn't sure whether to believe me or not. 'You're a seriously dark horse, Jem Clark. You could be sleeping with the guy and your own mother wouldn't know.'

You can bet on that, I thought as I collected my things before I left.

CHAPTER NINE

I WAS STILL running on caffeine when the doorbell rang to announce Alessandro's arrival. I opened the door to see him standing there with a bunch of creamy tea-roses. How on earth had he remembered I wasn't a red roses girl?

The delicacy, the subtle fragrance and the old-fashioned quality of those blooms took my breath away. I buried my head in the bouquet to disguise my reaction. Not that it worked. If I'd wanted to disguise how much his gesture meant to me I probably should have tossed them aside as if they were a bunch of cheap supermarket fragrance-free blooms. But it was too late now. I breathed in the gorgeous scent while the velvet-soft petals tickled my face.

'Your father is making an amazing recovery,' he said.

'Which he and my mother no doubt put down to the fact that they haven't eaten meat or been anywhere near a processed item of food in the last thirty-odd years,' I said.

He smiled. 'Your mother has been down to the kitchen and revamped the hospital menu—or at least tried to.'

I rolled my eyes and carried the roses to the sink, so I could put them in water before they could wilt.

'I had a breakthrough with Claudia today.'

'So she said.'

I swung around to face him. 'You've seen her?'

'I called in to the boarding house on my way past,' he said. 'She was just getting ready for bed. She told me about the drama lesson. She loved it, by the way.'

I turned on the tap to fill the vase I'd selected. *Selected?* Snort. I only had one. Just shows how often anyone brings me flowers. I made a little fuss over the way the blooms were positioned rather than look at him. I had a feeling he was getting far too good at reading me.

'She was a natural,' I said. 'She didn't stutter at all. I want her to take the lead role in the end-of-term play. It'll be great for her confidence. I just know she'll be brilliant.'

He came up behind me, put his hands on my shoulders and turned me. His eyes held mine with such warmth I felt something slip inside my stomach.

'I don't know how to thank you for what you're doing.'

'Yes, well—when it comes to thanks, what about what you did today?' I countered. 'You saved my father's life.'

He shrugged one of his shoulders. 'Any decent cardiac surgeon could've done that.'

I reached up with my hand and stroked his stubble-covered jaw. 'Yes, but *you* did it—and then drove all the way back down here to call in on Claudia and catch up with me.'

'Ah, yes, but I have an ulterior motive when it comes to you.'

'Let me guess. You want to get laid?'

He cupped my face in both his hands, his expression so darkly serious and intent it made something inside my chest quiver like a moth was trapped between my ribs.

'I don't want to pressure you into something you're not ready for,' he said, in that gravel-and-honey tone.

I'm ready! I wanted to shout. But the thirteen-year-old girl inside me appreciated his sensitivity. Oh, how she appreciated it! Adored it. Clung to it. Was healed by it.

'I want you,' I said, shocked at how much truth there was in that bald statement. I had never wanted anyone before him or since. I had no sex drive. Zero. Zilch. *Nada*. But when it came to him it was like a switch had been turned to 'on'. And not just on but flashing with neon lights.

I put my hands on the top of his shoulders, drawing him closer, feeling the heat of his aroused body next to my starving, aching one. 'Make love to me,' I said, in a whisper-soft voice.

His mouth came down and covered mine, fusing it with heat, with passion, and yet with such excruciating tenderness I felt tears gather at the back of my eyes. I kissed him back, with all the passion I had suppressed for so long. It came bursting out of me like a centuries-old fountain that had been blocked.

I heard him groan as our tongues met and tangled. I felt his erection surge against me as he gathered me closer. The heat that flared between us was like a wildfire. And yet he kept control of it. He held me as if I was a delicate bloom that would be bruised and crushed by rough handling.

I could feel my frozen heart melting, as if someone had aimed a laser-hot beam at it. I desperately tried to keep the crusty old armour that had guarded my heart for so long in place, but it was like trying to defend an ice cream cone from a naked flame. I was oozing with feeling. With feelings I'd locked away for years.

He kissed my mouth with aching tenderness. Then he trailed his mouth down my neck, lingering over my collarbone, moving to the valley of my cleavage. His tongue lit a fire beneath my flesh, making every nerve go off like a firecracker. I could feel that racing river of fire running along my nerve-endings. It was running out of control—along with my pulse.

His hands moved down my body, skating over my breasts without lingering. I wanted more. I wanted him to possess them, to palpate them as he had done in the past. I whimpered and pressed closer, urging him to take things to the next level.

He put his hands on my hips, holding me to his arousal. Letting me know how much he wanted me and yet letting me set the pace. There was no pressure. Not like I'd felt in the past. Wasn't that why I had struggled with anyone else as a sexual partner? I had never trusted them. I had never trusted them to gauge when I was out of my comfort zone.

Only Alessandro had done that. Had intuited that even without knowing what had happened to me.

I moaned with approval against his mouth as it covered mine again. I opened it to welcome his tongue back in, stroked mine along it and around it, sucking on it to make him aware of how much I wanted him.

He made a similar sound of approval as he released my hair from its tie. It cascaded around my shoulders and he took a handful of it as he angled my head for a deeper kiss.

I got to work on his clothes, but my fingers were in too much of a hurry. His hands came to the rescue, releasing buttons so I could slide my hands over the sexy planes and contours of his chest. He had just the right amount of chest hair. Call me old-fashioned, but I love a man who isn't 'manscaped'. My fingers spread through those tight whorls and then I pressed my mouth to his sternum, running my tongue down and then over and around each of his flat nipples.

He tipped my head back up and slowly slid my shirt off my shoulders, revealing just enough skin for his mouth to tease and tempt. I shivered as his lips moved over my bare flesh. My nipples tightened in anticipation inside the lacy cups of my bra. He slid the strap of my bra over my shoulder and trailed his hot mouth over the upper curve of my breast.

He didn't go anywhere near my nipple. He explored every other slope, leaving me in a state of frenzied sexual excitement. I pushed myself towards him. Wanton, I know, but I was going to die if he didn't take my breast—or what he could get of it—in his mouth.

And then he did it.

It was just as breathtaking as I remembered. Maybe even more so. His lips closed around my nipple, softly at first—a teasing little touch that made my sensitive nerves go haywire. Then he used his teeth in a light graze that made the hairs on the back of my neck dance at their roots. He did the same thing to my other breast, his touch so mind-blowing, I whimpered in delight.

He kissed his way back to my mouth, subjecting it to another passionate exchange that made my inner core coil with want. I put my arms around his neck, linking them behind his head, kissing him with such vigour I could feel the rasp of his stubble on my chin.

He eased back and lifted me in his arms, then carried me to the bedroom. You might wonder how he knew which one was mine, but the detritus of my parents' aborted stay was still evident in the spare room. I hadn't had the time or the inclination to clean it up.

Alessandro laid me down on the bed, but he didn't come down on top of me as he might have done in the past. He sat to one side of me, stroked my face as if I were young child.

'Are you sure you want to do this?' he said.

'What part of *I want you* are you not getting?' I said, tugging at the collar of his shirt so his head came down.

He kissed me softly as he joined me on the bed.

We were still wearing way too many clothes. I started on his trousers and he got working on mine. It was a mutual journey of discovery. I loved finding him again—the heat and strength and potent power of him springing out from the confines of his underwear made something deep in my core shudder in rapture.

He slowly peeled away my clothes until I was just in my knickers. Thankfully they were my best ones. Bertie bought them for me a couple of birthdays ago, but I'd pushed them to the back of the drawer as I thought they were too girly and feminine for me. They were black lace, with little pink bows on the hips.

Alessandro obviously liked them. I saw his eyes darken as he stroked his finger down the seam of my body. The sensation of his touch through the almost sheer lace made my back arch off the bed. I could feel my dampness. I was sure he could too as he gently peeled the lace away from my body and brought his mouth down.

I shivered all over as his lips touched me. I wished I'd had time to wax, but he didn't seem to mind. He separated me so tenderly; worshipping me with such achingly poignant reverence I had to blink back tears.

I realised then that he was my first lover in all the ways that counted. He had shown me how to experience pleasure. He had shown me what my body was capable of, how it responded to touch and carefully timed caresses. He had never touched me in a way I wasn't comfortable with. He had always treated me with the utmost respect and consideration. He had not selfishly satisfied his needs with no thought to mine.

He must have sensed my emotional response, for he stopped his gentle ministrations and came back up to look deeply into my eyes.

'Too much?'

I bit my lip and shook my head, suddenly incapable of speech.

He stroked the underside of my chin. 'I've given you beard rash.'

I could feel my chin wobbling, so I bit down even harder on my lip. His hand cradled my cheek, his eyes so dark and meltingly soft I knew I was a goner.

'You have the most beautiful mouth,' he said, stroking my bottom lip so I could no longer savage it. 'So soft...so sweet.'

'I like yours too.' My voice was so husky it didn't sound like me at all.

He kissed me again, softly and leisurely, until he sensed I was ready to continue. I let my body do the talking because it was easier that way. I didn't want to suddenly blurt out how much I'd missed him or how great he made me feel—how I wished we could rewind the past and do things differently. I just wanted to be as close to him as physically possible. I wanted to lose myself in his body, to feel the magnificence of sexual pleasure with him—only with him. I wanted to break free, to escape from everything that had been so tightly bound up inside me like a giant, prickly ball of bitterness.

Alessandro moved down my body again, taking me on a sensual quest that unmoored me from my foundations. I could feel myself being shaken loose with each stroke and flutter of his tongue against my hungry, aching, greedy flesh. The tremors of feeling moved through me until I was rolling, crashing like a wave against a shore. I was washed over with the sensations. Flooded with them. Drowned in delight. And then floating like a bit of flotsam in that blessed afterglow of release.

But I didn't want to be the only one to experience such amazing sensations. I wanted to give pleasure to him. It was my gift—the only thing I had to give him. I could no longer—*would* no longer—give him my heart, but my body was his for the asking.

I moved my hand down his shaft, rediscovering the shape and heft of him. Delighting in the way he sucked in a sharp-sounding breath, as if my touch ignited him like no other. His skin was silky and smooth, and yet the weight and thickness of him was as strong as steel. My body quivered with the memory of how it had felt to have him thrust inside me, losing himself in me.

He was fighting to control himself. I could feel the tension building in him. I could hear the hectic pace of his breathing as his need for release increased.

'Wait.'

He suddenly pulled back and reached over the side of the bed for his discarded trousers. I was glad one of us was being responsible about safe sex, because I can tell you right then it was the furthest thing from my mind. But I appreciated his concern—particularly as I wasn't currently taking the pill. I hadn't seen the need to pump myself full of hormones when I was basically celibate.

Alessandro came back safely sheathed and poised himself at my entrance. But still he didn't rush for completion. He caressed my breasts, using his hands, his lips and his tongue. He moved down my body, leaving a trail of blistering heat in his wake. I felt the pressure building inside me again as he came to my pubic bone. My nerve-endings began to twitch as his mouth came inexorably closer. I felt the warm gust of his breath against my labia, then the gentle glide of one of his fingers as he tested my moisture to see if I was ready for him.

I guided him with my hand, lifting my pelvis, making a pleading noise that was unintelligible but crossed all language barriers. He knew what I wanted and he gave it.

I gasped as he took that first slow but sure thrust. He could have gone much deeper and much harder, but he didn't. The measured pace was just right for me to find my own rhythm before I tried to keep up with his.

And then it all fell magically into place.

Somehow it was like beautiful choreography—a ballet of limbs and lips and lust and longing that built to a stunning, heart-stopping climax.

I closed my eyes to give myself up fully to the storm of passion that ricocheted through me. Tiny bright lights like a fistful of carelessly flung diamonds sparkled behind my eyelids. My flesh tingled from head to foot and my heart raced in time with Alessandro's. I could feel it pumping against my crushed breasts, where his body was pressed as the final waves of release washed over him.

I could have used one or two of Bertie's 'wows' just then, but I decided to stay silent. Talking would break the spell that had fallen around and over us like a velvet blanket.

My fingers started moving up and down the length of his strong spine like a lapsed pianist working on her scales.

'"Twinkle, Twinkle, Little Star"?' Alessandro said after a moment, his voice a deep rumble against my neck, where his face was pressed.

I couldn't stop a laugh escaping. 'Good guess. How about this one?' I tapped out the rhythm to 'Three Blind Mice'.

I felt his lips move against my neck as he spoke. 'Play it again.'

I played it again, slower this time. 'Come on,' I said, laughing again. 'It's an easy one.'

His lips started to nibble on my earlobe. 'Give me a clue.'

I shivered all over as his tongue traced the cartilage of ear. My fingers stopped playing their tune and started weaving their way through the thickness of his hair. 'I'm tired of that game,' I said in a breathy whisper. 'Let's play something else.'

He propped himself up on his elbows, his eyes glinting at me smoulderingly. 'Any suggestions?'

I circled his mouth with one of my fingertips, the

sound of his skin rasping against mine making something topple inside my belly. 'Three Questions?'

He lifted one dark eyebrow. 'I haven't heard of that game. How does it go?'

I traced the right angle of his jaw with my finger. 'I get to ask you three questions. Anything I want. And you have to answer.'

A flicker of tension passed across his cheek before he got it under control. 'And do I get to ask *you* three questions of my choice too?'

'Of course.'

Now, you might ask why I was playing such a potentially dangerous game, but I had already told him my worst secret. What did I have to lose? Besides, I had a feeling there was something he wasn't telling me about his sister Bianca. Don't ask me how I knew. I'm not psychic…or at least I hope not.

'O-kay,' he said, but his tone was unmistakably cautious.

'What's the most difficult operation you've ever done?' No point in starting with the big one, I thought. I'd work up to it.

He didn't hesitate in answering. 'It was a heart transplant on a seventeen-year-old when I was a registrar. Things didn't go according to plan. To be fair, it was a risky case. But the consultant was one of those instrument-throwing ones. He was out of his depth but refused to admit it. He sent me out to tell the relatives their son hadn't made it. I'll never forget their faces. They leapt to their feet, eager for good news, and I had to tell them the opposite.'

I looked at his face, saw the anguish of that remembered tragic encounter playing out over his features—

the shadows in his eyes, the ghosts of lost patients who lingered to haunt him. 'That must have been awful for them—and for you,' I said. 'And cowardly of the consultant to leave it up to you.'

He brushed a stray strand of hair away from my face. 'It was a good lesson to learn. I make a point of dealing directly with relatives. Not to mention keeping a cool head under pressure. Things *can* go wrong. No one—no matter how skilled or how much experience they have—is exempt from that. But staying calm in the middle of a crisis can be the difference between life and death.'

Somehow we had shifted our bodies so we were lying side by side, one of his legs draped over one of mine, our hands loosely entwined.

'Next question?'

I had to remind myself of the game. I was so taken aback by the quality of him, the strength and courage he exhibited under pressure. Was that why he hadn't acted the way I'd expected when I'd accused him of using me five years ago? He had faced down my spitting tirade with what I'd thought was cool indifference. But what if that had been his way of keeping calm when the unexpected was thrown at him?

It was a sobering thought.

'Did you have a pet as a child?' I said.

A shadow passed over his features like a cloud crossing the path of the moon. 'Yes. His name was Cico.'

'What happened to him?'

'He died.'

'When?'

'That's question number four,' he said. 'Now it's my turn.'

'Hang on a minute.' I gave his chest a playful shove. 'I want to know what happened to him.'

Alessandro captured my hand and came back over me, all but pinning me to the bed. 'You're the one who made the rules, *ma petite*. You can't go changing them now.'

I gave up with good grace...well, good for me—if you overlook the quick tongue poke and the childish pout. 'Okay, fire away,' I said.

'Do you want to have dinner or make love again?'

'Make love.'

He smiled and brought his head down. I grabbed a fistful of his hair and pulled him away from his mission.

'Hang on. Don't you want to ask another two questions?' I said.

'I'm getting to that.' He sent his mouth on a hot trail down to my breasts. 'Does that feel good?'

'Yes...' It was part gasp, part groan.

He moved down my body and kissed the sensitive skin of my inner thigh. 'How about that?'

Somehow I lost count of the questions, and suddenly I was incapable of answering. Anything.

CHAPTER TEN

MY FATHER MADE a spectacular recovery—which, as I'd predicted, my mother and to some degree my father took all the credit for. However, they *did* think to organise a thank-you card for Alessandro and a bottle of wine. It wasn't a top-shelf one, but it was organic.

They came back to my place to collect their things, but they didn't hang around.

I was awkward with my mother. Nothing new there, but now there was another layer of awkwardness. She obviously hadn't said anything to my father about our discussion/argument, which showed at least she had *some* sensitivity, given he was still getting over heart surgery. But I had a feeling she might never tell him. She would do what she had always done when things got too confrontational or threatening for her. She would bury her head in the sand, or in her navel, or take up with yet another guru to distract herself from facing reality.

I stood on my front step and waved my parents off, feeling that mixture of guilt and relief that so perplexed and frustrated me.

They had not long gone when I heard the unmistakable roar of Alessandro's car turning the corner.

I couldn't wait to tell him how well Claudia was

doing. The drama therapy was going gangbusters. Even the speech therapist was stunned by Claudia's progress in such a short space of time. Although Claudia's stutter was still present, the boost in her confidence from doing those drama exercises had helped her to be not so distressed about the words and sounds she couldn't say, but to concentrate on what she could.

The only thing that still troubled me now was how she never mentioned her mother. It was unusual in a child so young. She didn't show any signs of homesickness either. She had settled into the boarding house routine as if she'd been boarding for years. That sort of quiet self-reliance in an older child would have been laudable. However, in a child of Claudia's age it was faintly disturbing.

But then I thought of my tricky relationship with *my* mother. Kids soon learn who they can rely on and make the necessary adjustments. I for one knew all about making adjustments. I swear I could moonlight as a spanner.

I watched as Alessandro's powerful car growled into one of the few parking spaces at the front of my flat. He had spent the last few days working in London. I knew he was finding it tough, balancing his supervision of the renovations on his house here in Bath and his commitment to his niece, not to mention our 'relationship'— which I automatically put in quotation marks because I didn't know what else to call it.

It didn't feel like a fling, but neither did it feel like a proper commitment. He had made it clear he wasn't able to offer anything permanent, and I had made it equally clear I didn't want to settle down. The trouble was I was having wayward thoughts that would catch me totally off guard.

Like when I went to my wardrobe to get dressed for school and my wedding dress, hidden in its silk bag, kind of stared at me. For all that it was covered in a sack—hidden, stashed away—it had an annoying habit of reminding me of the hopes and dreams I had once clung to. It was like I had shoved a part of myself into the dark recesses of my wardrobe but now that part was getting restless…agitated.

I decided I would give the damn dress away or stuff it in a charity bin the first chance I got.

As Alessandro walked towards me from his car, I could see he wasn't having the best of days. His eyes had dark circles beneath them and his skin looked too tightly drawn over his face. And there I was thinking teaching was stressful. At least I had never had to tell a parent their kid had died under my care.

'Tough day slaving over a hot pericardium?' I said.

The corners of his mouth lifted in a half smile. 'No surgery today—just a clinic that went on for ages.'

He bent down and pressed a kiss to my lips. I breathed in the tangy citrus scent of him and my senses spun as his mouth increased its pressure. He made a low, deep sound and put his arms around me, drawing me to him until our bodies were flush against each other. Somehow him hugging me or me hugging him wasn't a problem for me. We fitted together like two pieces of one of those complicated Mensa puzzles.

I wondered what my neighbours would make of it. I normally lived such a boring, uneventful life that for them to see a handsome man drive up in a top-model Maserati and take me in his arms and kiss me soundly was probably much better viewing than what was currently on the television. Out of the corner of my eye

I saw a couple of curtains twitch, which more or less confirmed my suspicions. Honestly. Some people need to get a life.

Alessandro raised his mouth just high enough to speak. 'It is just me, or do you get the feeling we're being watched?'

'Maybe we should go inside and let their imaginations take over?' I said.

He brushed his lips across mine again. 'Good plan.'

I must have fallen asleep after we made love, because I woke to find Alessandro sitting on the edge of my bed watching me. He was fully dressed, which wasn't how I'd left him. He had even put some order to his hair— presumably with his fingers, for I could see the track marks in between those jet-black strands.

I pushed myself up on my elbows and shook my head so my hair went back behind my shoulders. 'You're leaving?' I tried to strip my voice of any trace of disappointment, but I'm not sure I managed it.

He trailed an idle finger down the slope of my cheek. 'What are you doing next weekend?'

A big fat nothing—just like I did every weekend. But I didn't want to admit that. I didn't want to sound too eager. I didn't want to appear too available. A girl had her pride, after all.

'I have a couple of things on,' I said. 'Why?'

A frown had formed a crease on his forehead. 'The school is shut next weekend, and I still haven't found a suitable nanny for Claudia.'

I could see where this was going and stayed silent. My sister is the opposite with silences. She hates them. She babbles whatever comes into her head if there's one to fill. I am more for waiting to see how long it takes for the other person to get to the point.

Alessandro got to the point a whole lot faster than most.

'Would you be able to do it? Look after her for the weekend? I should be back late on Saturday night. I have a commitment in London. I have to be there. It's a research meeting I've had booked for months. If I pull out, the project could fall over.'

I looked at where his hand was resting on the bed, within touching distance of mine. I could feel the magnetic force of it. It was all I could do not to reach out and touch him.

I brought my gaze up to his. 'Will she want to come and stay with me?'

His tense features visibly relaxed. 'She'll love it. She talks about you all the time.'

I lifted my eyebrows. 'Talks?'

He smiled. 'Yes. Talks. With the occasional stutter, but at least she's talking.'

I dragged at my lower lip with my teeth and glanced at our hands, so close but still not touching. Was he feeling the same gravitational pull as I was?

'Yes, she's come ahead in leaps and bounds, but there's one thing that troubles me...' I looked into his eyes again. 'She never mentions her mother. *Never*. It's as if she's forgotten she *has* a mother or is deliberately *not* thinking about her. Why is that?'

He let out a long sigh as he sent one of his hands through his hair. 'I suspect Claudia has learnt from an early age that she can't always rely on her mother,' he said. 'It's as if she knows Bianca is incapable of being present emotionally, even if she's able to be there physically—although of course just now that's impossible.'

I slipped my hand over his and gave it a gentle squeeze. 'What's wrong with Bianca? I mean apart from the drug problem?'

He looked at me—such a bleak look that I felt my chest tighten as if it was caught in a vice.

'She's had a mental breakdown,' he said. 'I think it's been coming on for months—years, more like. I had to have her sectioned. In layman's terms that means admitted to a mental health facility for her own safety.'

I swallowed and gripped his hand a little tighter. 'I know what it means... I'm so sorry...'

His fingers somehow turned, so that it was his hand holding mine. 'My priority is to keep Claudia safe, no matter what.'

'Hence my school?'

His eyes met mine. 'I knew you would be the one person I could rely on to make sure my niece got the care and attention she needed,' he said. 'I'm not an expert on small children. I've got my sister's situation to prove that.'

I frowned at him. 'Why are you blaming yourself? Your sister's problems have nothing to do with you. Mental illness can be due to so many factors. Genetics or—'

He got up so abruptly from the bed that I stopped speaking. It was like a guillotine had come down on my sentence.

'They have *everything* to do with me,' he said as he paced the small area of floor available. 'I blame myself. I should've seen the signs.'

I rolled my lips together, shocked at how dry they had suddenly become. I didn't fill the silence. I have a feeling even Bertie the obsessive silence filler would have left this one open, for Alessandro to continue when he was good and ready.

He turned and looked at me with a harrowed look. 'My father is responsible for Bianca's problems. All of them. Every single one.'

I felt my throat move over another tight swallow. 'Was he…violent towards her too?'

'It depends what you mean by violence.'

He turned away from me, to inspect something on my dressing table. I knew it wasn't that he was interested in my hairbrush or the perfume atomiser. He was gathering himself. Drawing on his inner reserve to contain the anger he felt against his father.

And then suddenly I got it.

The ugliness of it crept into the silence like a loathsome creature, reaching out with long, slithering tentacles to strangle every atom of oxygen out of the room.

'He sexually abused her.'

I didn't say it as a question. I didn't need to. The ghastly truth was written on Alessandro's face when I met his eyes in my dressing table mirror.

He turned and faced me. 'I only found out a month ago. It explained everything. Her rebellion during her childhood and teens, the drugs, the drink, the promiscuous behaviour.' He dragged a hand down his face, momentarily distorting his features. 'I could have stopped it if I'd known earlier. I *would* have stopped it. I would've made sure he was sent to rot in prison. But she didn't tell me.'

'When did the abuse start?'

'It started when we were sent to live with him, after our mother died. He groomed her for years. I can never

forgive myself for not protecting her. Now he's denying everything and he's got himself a hot-shot defence
lawyer who'll pull apart my sister's life until they take
everything away from her—including Claudia.'

My heart ached for Alessandro's sister. I was all too
well aware of the silence of shame that could go on for
decades. I thought of her as a motherless little girl, un-
able to protect herself. Alessandro was blaming himself, but he'd been a kid too. How could he have possibly
known what was going on? Perpetrators made sure such
dirty secrets remained secret. It was part of the power
they had over their victims.

'A lot of victims find it very difficult to speak of
what's happened to them—even to those closest to
them,' I said. 'And when the abuse has been happen-
ing for a long time, and from a young age...well, there
are other factors. Fear of not being believed. Fear of re-
prisal from the perpetrator. It's terribly complex. The
fact is you know now. So you can keep her and Claudia
safe—which you're doing to the best of your ability.'

One of his hands pushed through his hair. 'I couldn't
even keep a *dog* safe from him. What hope did I have
to keep my sister safe?'

My stomach clenched. Cico. The dog Alessandro
had mentioned when we played Three Questions. *Oh,
dear God.* What a ghastly childhood he'd had. I felt a
sudden rush of shame for all the times I'd criticised my
parents. There were far worse things than having hippie parents. Far, *far* worse.

Alessandro came over and sat beside me on the bed
again. He put his hand over mine. 'I want to help my
sister move beyond this,' he said. 'I want her to be a
proper mother to Claudia. I want justice for her. But

she's not strong enough to cope with the judicial system. I'm worried if I push too hard she'll do something even more drastic than she's already done.'

I turned my hand over and curled my fingers around his. 'You're doing all you can. If and when she feels ready to press charges then you'll be by her side to help her through it. If she can't face it then you have to accept that. It's her choice. It *has* to be her choice.'

His thumb moved back and forth across my index finger tendon. 'Did *you* ever consider pressing charges?'

I dropped my gaze to where our hands were joined.

'For a long while I pretended it hadn't happened. I blocked it out. I refused to think about it. I didn't want it to define me. It's too late now anyway. It would be his word against mine. We were both kids without the proper guidance of responsible parents. Why would I put myself through it? I have better things to do.'

He eased up my chin so our eyes could meet. 'You must never blame yourself.'

'I don't,' I said. 'Men like that boy and your father are pond scum. They'll get what's coming to them eventually—at least that's what I hope.'

He let out another long breath and laid my hand back down on the bedcovers. 'I have to get going. I have a couple of things to check at my house.'

Take me with you.

The words were on the tip of my tongue but I closed my lips over them. No point in imagining a romantic candlelit picnic in his gorgeous old house. No point in imagining he might want to spend the whole night with me instead of a couple of hours. No point imagining anything other than what we had here and now. Sex without strings. Without commitment. A day-by-day affair.

I waited a beat before saying, 'I'll bring Claudia home with me on Friday after school. There'll be paperwork for you to sign, to give me authority. Can you drop by the school office in the next day or so?'

'Sure.'

He leaned closer to press a soft kiss to my lips. I was so tempted to lengthen the contact with him but I needed to keep perspective. We had already crossed a few boundaries I had never crossed with anyone before. The deep and meaningful—and painful—conversations were a totally new thing for me.

I suspected they were a new thing for him too.

Claudia was clearly excited about coming home with me the following Friday, but was trying her best not to show it. Her big brown eyes followed me all day during class time with a distinctive gleam. Every time I caught her looking at me her little cheeks would blush as red as an apple. She would bury her chin into her neck, or hunch over her desk and pretend to be busy with whatever task I had set.

The thought of her being pleased about spending the weekend with me thrilled me in a way I had not expected to feel. Don't get me wrong. I have the occasional child I warm to, in spite of all of my efforts to avoid playing favourites. But there was something about Claudia that awoke a dormant mothering instinct in me.

Ever since I had broken up with Alessandro I had put all thoughts of motherhood aside. I had drawn a line through it with a thick red pen like someone does on a mistake in a document. I had erased it. Deleted it. But like indelible ink it was seeping back into my focus.

I was nearly thirty years old. I didn't even have a cat to go home to. I used to have a rat once, but Bertie hates them and they're not exactly the easiest pet to farm out when you want to go on holiday. No amount of telling people how intelligent rats are has ever overcome their image problem. Sad, but true.

Claudia's lack of mothering reminded me of my issues with *my* mother. I know mothers take the rap for a lot of the world's problems—which is grossly unfair because it takes two to make a child—but kids need someone watching out for them. They need to feel secure in the knowledge that someone is there for them, no matter what.

Claudia had gravitated towards me even though she had an uncle who clearly adored her. But Alessandro had work pressures and concerns about his sister—Claudia's mother. I wondered if Claudia had turned to me because I was someone she saw each day...someone who was reliable and consistent and there for her no matter what.

I hadn't seen Alessandro since he'd organised the paperwork to allow me to take Claudia home with me. He had been called away to London over a patient who had developed a complication after a stent insertion. I was becoming more and more aware of the stresses he was under. It's not that I hadn't thought about it before—over the years I'd seen the sort of pressures Bertie had been under in her work as an anaesthetist. When she puts people to sleep she wants them to wake up. When Alessandro operates on someone he wants them to get better.

The tragic reality is not everyone does.

* * *

Finally it was time to leave school. I went over to the boarding house to find Claudia with a little overnight case packed and sitting on her bed, swinging her legs as if she couldn't keep still.

'Ready?' I said.

She nodded and jumped off the bed, and went to pick up her bag from where it was on the floor.

'Here,' I said, and reached for it. 'Let me take it for you. It looks heavy.'

It wasn't—but I wondered wryly if I would turn out to be one of those musical-instrument-and-sports-equipment-carrying parents I had so roundly criticised.

You're not going to be a parent.

The internal voice was a jarring reminder of the obdurate stance I had taken as a result of my heartbreak. Five years on and I was still punishing myself for being naive. I was denying myself a lifetime of joy and fulfilment because I had been let down by a man who hadn't loved me the way I thought he should have.

But the more I knew of Alessandro the more I worried that I might have got it wrong about him. He was not a man to turn his back on responsibility or a commitment he had made to someone.

Yes, we'd had a whirlwind affair, but people *did* fall in love quickly. It wasn't unusual. Sometimes the most passionate and enduring relationships were the result of instant attraction.

And it didn't come much more instant that ours.

I had allowed bitterness to cloud my judgement. Not only bitterness—insecurity. Loads and loads of insecurity. I swear if anyone knew how much baggage I was carrying around I'd be charged extra on flights.

I had always thought of myself as damaged goods. It was what I'd believed since I was thirteen years old. I wasn't worthy. I didn't deserve to have it all because I felt it had all been taken away from me.

But what if I could get myself to the stage of wanting it all again? Believing I was not only worthy of it but actively *seeking* it? Expressing my needs without fear of rejection or ridicule?

Scary thought.

Claudia was silent for most of the journey to my flat. But then, just as I pulled into the one available space on my street, she turned to me and asked, 'Are you going to marry Un-c-c-c-le Alessandro?'

My chest gave a tight squeeze as she struggled over the word 'uncle'. The hard consonants were still a problem for her, but at least she wasn't avoiding saying them. 'What makes you ask that?' I said, in the most casual tone I could muster.

She gave a little shrug that would have looked out of place on a sixteen-year-old, let alone a six-year-old. 'Just wondering.'

'We're…friends.'

Her big brown eyes were trained on me. '*Best* friends?'

I opened my mouth and then closed it. I had told Alessandro more than I had told anyone. *Ever.* Not even my sister, Bertie, had been privy to my darkest secrets. Did that make him and me best friends?

'Why don't you ask him?' I said.

'I will.'

Another scary thought.

CHAPTER ELEVEN

I closed the book I had been reading to Claudia as a bedtime story and set it on the bedside table in my spare room. I'd read the same story to her four times because she'd said it was her favourite.

The Three Billy Goats Gruff was a favourite of mine when I was a kid too. To tell you the truth it's still a favourite. Particularly since the advent of social media, where there are more trolls around than ever.

But don't get me started.

I watched Claudia's dark spider-leg-like lashes resting on her cheeks. Her soft little rosebud mouth was parted slightly as she drifted into deep sleep. I had the most compelling urge to press a kiss to her little forehead.

Teachers these days aren't supposed to have unnecessary physical contact with their pupils.

But right then I didn't feel like her teacher.

We'd decided she was to call me Jem while she was with me. She would have to go back to addressing me as Miss Clark when she was at school. But I didn't want her to be worried the whole weekend about her lisp and her stutter.

I tiptoed out of the spare room and gently closed

the door. I had a sudden flashback to when my mother would sometimes tell Bertie and me a story when she put us to bed…or whatever it was we were sleeping on during that phase of our lives. I seem to remember a hammock at one point, and a yoga mat on the floor of a circus-sized tent.

My mother didn't read the standard children's books of the day. No way. She made stuff up. Fantastical stuff—whimsical tales that went on and on until Bertie and I were roaring with laughter at the absurdity of the characters and their adventures and mishaps. She even let us offer alternative endings. That had been so much fun.

How could I have forgotten those times? It was so easy to concentrate on the bad things, the times when things hadn't felt right for me, but there were many times when things had been good.

I had never felt unloved. I had never been abused in any way. I had never been smacked. I had never been spoken to with harsh or punitive or shaming words. I had long lamented and criticised the lack of structure in our lives, but I had overlooked the benefits of being allowed to find my own personal boundaries. I hadn't had control and discipline enforced upon me externally. I had been allowed to develop it internally, which surely was far more powerful and lasting.

I looked at my phone, lying on the kitchen bench. Actually, it sort of looked at me—a bit like my wedding dress. Should I call my mother and apologise? I chewed at my lip. I hate apologising. I hate being wrong. Call it pride. Call it stubbornness. Call it avoidance. I had climbed so far up on my high horse I had vertigo.

But before I could call my mother, my phone started

to ring. It was Bertie, who'd called to tell me about a bridesmaid dress fitting.

'I hope you're not going to make me wear some frothy, frilly thing I'll never be able to wear again?' I said.

'I've got a lovely design picked out,' Bertie said. 'How do you feel about pink?'

'What shade of pink?'

'Hot pink. Fluorescent hot.'

I smothered a groan. 'You're going to make me wear fluorescent hot pink and stand in front of how many people, for how many hours, with a rictus smile on my face for all the photographs? That's taking sisterly love *way* too far.'

Bertie giggled. 'Just wait till Alessandro sees you in it. He'll be knocked sideways.'

'What makes you think *he's* going to see me in it?' I said.

'You'll bring him to the wedding, won't you?'

'Why would I do that?'

'Because you're seeing him.'

'Your wedding is four months away,' I said. 'He hasn't had a relationship last longer than a month since we broke up five years ago.'

'Isn't that telling you something?'

'Yes—he's a playboy who doesn't want to settle down,' I said. 'He's told me he's not in it for the long haul. But then neither am I.'

Bertie made a tut-tutting noise.

'What?' I said.

'You're going to end up one of those crazy old ladies with a hundred cats for company in her dotage.'

'Maybe I'll have rats.'

'Euueew!' Bertie said, and then quickly changed the subject. 'So, what are you doing this weekend? Are you seeing Alessandro?'

'I'm minding his niece.'

'Wow!'

'There's nothing "wow" about it,' I said. 'He's got a research meeting in London and the school is closed. Claudia has nowhere else to go. It's the least I could do. She's a great little kid. No trouble at all.'

'Wow.'

'Will you stop it with the "wows", already?' I said.

'So when will you see him again?'

'Late tomorrow night, if he gets back in time, or maybe Sunday.'

'Are you in love with him?'

'Why are you asking me such a ridiculous question?' I said.

Bertie gave a dreamy-sounding sigh. 'I thought so.'

'You *thought* so?' I said. 'What's that supposed to mean?'

'I have to go,' Bertie said. 'Matt's just got back from the hospital. We're heading out for dinner. 'Bye-ee!'

I stared at my phone's blank screen for a moment before putting it on the coffee table. I had barely sat back against the sofa cushions when it rang again and the screen indicated it was Alessandro.

I put on my cool and businesslike voice as I answered it. 'Jem Clark speaking.'

'Hi.'

I wasn't sure how he could make one syllable of greeting sound so sexy, but he did. I felt a shivery frisson go right through my body. 'Hello,' I said. 'Did you want to talk to Claudia? I'm sorry—she's fast asleep.

She stayed up later than normal, because it's not a school night, but—'

'I should've called earlier but I was held up in Theatre.'

'It's fine—she understands,' I said. 'We've talked about your job. She likes the fact you save lives. It gives her street cred with the other girls. Not every girl has a famous uncle.'

'Has she talked about her mother?'

'A little.'

'What did she say?'

'It was when we were choosing a book to read before bed,' I said. 'She told me her mother used to read to her at night. I got the feeling it was quite a while ago. I didn't press her on it. I figure she'll talk when she's ready to talk.'

'Thanks again for minding her. I'm not sure how to make it up to you.'

'It's not a problem—really. She's an angel.'

There was a little silence. But then I heard a phone or a pager ringing in the background.

'Sorry, Jem,' he said. 'I have to go. I'll call you tomorrow if I get held up. *Ciao*.'

I looked at my blank screen for the second time that evening. ''Bye,' I said, and sat back against the sofa cushions with a sigh.

I spent a fun day on Saturday with Claudia. I had some grocery shopping to do in the morning, and Claudia seemed to enjoy helping me with it. I planned to do some baking with her during the afternoon, as it was something I'd missed out on as a child. My mother would have freaked out at the sight of white sugar, white flour and butter. I never got to lick the beaters or scrape out the bowl after making cupcakes or brownies.

Not that I'm bitter about it. *Much.* I really had to stop harping on about my mother. Anyone would think I needed a therapist. I still hadn't called her. My mother— not my therapist. I don't have one. But I was starting to think maybe I should.

After we dropped the shopping at home Claudia and I went for a walk to my favourite park, where we fed the ducks and ate a picnic lunch. Then we spent a lovely afternoon baking. The smells coming from my kitchen were amazing.

I had never really thought of my flat as a home before. It was just my accommodation. My place of residence. But filled with the smell of cupcakes and chocolate crunch slices and lemon meringue pies—I'd gone a little overboard on the sweet stuff, but Claudia didn't seem to mind—my flat began to feel like home. Especially with a little girl propped at my kitchen bench, with sticky hands and cake batter around her smiling mouth and a swipe of flour across her cheek.

I had another flashback. Mum and me at a campsite, with the warm glow of the fire and the smell of a delicious beany sort of curry that she was showing me how to cook. It was a Mum-and-me moment. We didn't have too many of them, as there were always a lot of other people around. It's like that in communes. No privacy. But that time we had the campfire to ourselves.

I can't remember how old I was…maybe seven or eight. But I do remember the way she made sure I wasn't too close to the hot coals—made sure I kept my sleeve away from the heat as I stirred the pot that was propped on the stones that surrounded the fire. I remember thinking at the time how many generations of people must have done that, from way back in primitive times to the present day. Cooked around a campfire. Swapped stories. Shared wisdom. Shared recipes for food, for life, for love.

I looked at my phone but didn't pick it up. The excuses were there, like scouts turning up for a parade. The kitchen was a mess. My arms were up to the elbows in flour. I had Claudia to mind. I had a cake just about ready to come out of the oven.

Truth was—I was a coward.

I think it was all the sugar that made Claudia resist going to bed that night. Or maybe it was because she was hoping her uncle would make it back in time to say goodnight before she went to bed.

I'd read several stories, and even made up one or two of my own, thinking of my mother with a sharp little pang. But after a while I realised it was pointless unless Claudia was tired.

I left her playing with some of the toys I'd managed to salvage from my childhood. There wasn't much. My parents hadn't believed in giving Bertie and I gender-specific toys. We'd made our own out of sticks and twigs and bits of fabric—which, now that I thought about it, was pretty cool. Kids today get given so much they don't have to use their imaginations. Bertie and I had played shops with shells and stones and sea glass behind a sandcastle counter. It had been brilliant fun.

'Do you have a dress-up box?' Claudia asked when I went in to check on her after I'd done the dishes from supper.

'Give me a second,' I said, and went to my bedroom.

I heard the soft pad of her little feet following me. She was like a loyal little puppy, following its new owner. I couldn't help feeling chuffed that she'd bonded so well to me.

I slid the wardrobe door back just far enough to get out a pair of heels and a hippie kaftan my mother had given me for my birthday. Needless to say I had never worn it. It was a bright vomit-coloured swirl, but I thought Claudia wouldn't mind so long as it was long and floaty and grown-up. There was also a hat I'd worn to a friend's wedding, a couple of handbags and scarves, and a long string of fake pearls.

The satin bag with my wedding dress inside was still safely at the back of the wardrobe, still behind my hiking jacket. Even though I knew it would be the ultimate in dress-up for a six-year-old girl, I left it where it was.

The doorbell sounded, but Claudia was too engrossed in putting her tiny feet into a pair of my heels so I left her there while I answered it.

Alessandro was standing there, with a box of hand-made chocolates and another bunch of flowers. Lovely old-fashioned cottage flowers—white lilacs and blush-pink peonies that would have filled my flat with their gorgeous fragrance if it wasn't for the lingering smell of home baking.

I saw his nostrils dilate. 'You've been baking?'

'Guilty as charged.' I took the flowers from him with a smile. 'Claudia loved it. She was a great little assistant. I hardly needed to wash the beaters or the bowls after she'd been to work on them.'

His smile was warm, his dark brown eyes soft. 'Is she asleep now?'

I gave him a rolled-eye look. 'Yeah, well... Here's

the thing about baking with six-year-olds. She's in sugar overload. I couldn't get her to go to bed. She's still up playing.' I nodded my head in the direction of my room. 'Go in and say hello to her. I'll just find a jar or something to put these in.'

I sorted out the flowers and stepped back to inspect my handiwork. Yep. I was definitely improving in my flower-arranging skills.

I heard a sound behind me and turned from the flowers to see Claudia swishing into the room. I say 'swishing' because the voluminous folds of my wedding dress were swamping her tiny frame in spite of the pair of heels she'd put on.

She shuffled towards me with a big smile on her face. 'Look what I found in your wardrobe!' she crowed with excitement.

I didn't have the heart to burst her bubble by giving her a stern lecture about rummaging in other people's wardrobes without permission. Besides, her uncle was standing there with an unreadable expression on his face.

'Well, look at you,' I said. 'Don't you look gorgeous in my sister's wedding dress?'

I know. Lying to a little kid. How low could I go?

'Do you have a veil?' Claudia asked.

'No, I didn't buy—'

I realised my mistake halfway through the sentence. Alessandro was now looking at me with a frown, but I soldiered on regardless.

'I didn't buy one for her. *For my sister.* Yet. But I intend to. It's next on my list of things to do. We'll do it when we sort out my bridesmaid dress. Did I tell you I'm going to be her bridesmaid? My dress is pink. Hot pink. Not a colour I would have chosen for myself, but it's my sister's special day and I wouldn't want anything to spoil it.'

I was done.

I was out of breath, for one thing. My heart was hammering like a demented timepiece in my chest. I was sweating as if the temperature had risen forty degrees. I glanced again at Alessandro, but his expression was back to being indecipherable.

I gave Claudia a bright smile. 'Well, young lady, I think it might be time to make your uncle a nice cup of tea and see if he'd like to sample some of our baking. What do you think?'

It was a strange little tea party. I was on tenterhooks and overcompensating by talking too much. Bertie would have rolled about the floor laughing. Claudia had helped Alessandro to some lemon meringue pie and was chatting about how she had been allowed to whip up the egg whites for the meringue all by herself.

'It's delicious,' he said, smiling at her.

After a while Claudia tried to disguise a huge yawn. I was all for ignoring it, as I dreaded being alone with Alessandro once she was safely tucked in bed. But he was clearly of the opinion that adults needed time alone without the presence of young children. *Oh, joy.*

I was still in clean-up mode in the kitchen when he came back. My kitchen was spotless, but that didn't stop me. I was polishing every surface with an antibacterial spray like someone with severe OCD.

'We need to talk.'

'We do?' I took one look at him and put my spray bottle down. 'So, how was your research meeting? Did it all go to plan? Is your project secure? Do you have to ask for funding or is that already—?'

'Jem.'

I pressed my lips together and gripped the kitchen bench rather than face him. 'It's not what you think.'

'I've given you no promises,' he said. 'No guarantees. I've spelled it out for you in the bluntest terms possible. I'm not offering marriage.'

I let go of the bench to look at him. 'You think I bought that dress *recently*?'

His frown made his eyebrows meet over his eyes. 'Didn't you?'

I laughed.

I know. I sound like a complete nutcase. But I couldn't help it. The irony of it was amusing even though it was also tragic.

I finally got control of myself enough to speak. 'I bought it five years ago. Three days before we broke up, to be precise. I thought you were going to ask me to marry you. I was ridiculously naive, and I completely misread the signs because there was no way you were going—'

'I was.'

I blinked. I swallowed what felt like a fishhook stuck in my throat. 'You were?'

He scraped his hand through his hair. 'I was going to ask you to marry me because back then I could think of no one I would rather spend my life with than you...'

I could sense a big *but* coming.

He drew in a breath and let it out in a rush. 'But I realise I wasn't ready for that level of commitment. I was too career-focused. I didn't have the right priorities. Which was why all my other relationships had failed.'

'So what about now?'

I shouldn't have asked. I shouldn't have revealed any sign of my yearnings. The yearnings I hadn't even been able to admit to myself. Until now.

'Marriage is out of the question now.'

'Why?'

I couldn't believe I was flogging such a lame horse. It was nothing short of cruel.

A flicker of pain passed over his features. 'Don't you see?'

All I was seeing was a life devoid of happiness, with no intimacy, spending my end days with a house full of cats or rats or…budgerigars. I figured at least they could talk.

'What am I supposed to be seeing?' I said.

He closed his eyes for a moment. Shook his head. Opened his eyes again and gave me a grimace of a smile.

'You act so tough and street-wise and smart, but inside you're still that sweet, innocent girl outside that Paris café.'

Was I?

No-freaking-José-way!

'I'm not after marriage,' I said. 'I'm happy with a fling. We can fling all we like. No one is going to stop us.'

He came over and took me by the shoulders. 'You deserve more than a fling, *ma petite*. You deserve your day as a princess. You deserve to wear your pretty dress and dream of happy-ever-after. I can't give you that.'

I frowned. 'But you do care for me…don't you?'

He gave me such a wistful look, my chest seized.

'I have too many people in my life who need me

right now. My sister. Claudia. My patients. I'm not capable of giving you what you need. I can't juggle all of that *and* you.'

'I don't need to be juggled,' I said. 'I need to be loved. That's all I'm asking for.'

I couldn't believe I was asking. Make that *begging*.

His hands fell from my shoulders. His expression was painful to witness. He wore his determination, his sense of responsibility and his inner loneliness like scars carved deeply into his features.

'Sometimes love isn't enough.'

'Is this about your father?' I asked. 'Are you worried about turning out like—?'

'No.'

'You're nothing like him,' I said. 'You could *never* be like him.'

'It's not about my father. It's about me. I can't do it and fail. It would hurt too many people. I don't want that on my conscience as well as everything else.'

'Why do you think you'll fail?'

I was all fired up. I had put my heart on the line. I had nothing to lose. Well, I had *everything* to lose— but I wasn't able to stop myself from being honest and up-front.

'You and I belong together. We're a great team. Look at how well we handle little Claudia. Your sister would always have us at her back, to step in if she couldn't cope. We could have our *own* children. We could build a life together. Can't you see that?'

His face had that boxed-up look I dreaded. The drawbridge was up. The subject was closed. He had made up his mind.

'I can't marry you, Jem,' he said. 'I'm sorry. Any relationship between us has to be informal. Casual. That's all I can offer.'

'I want more.'

I was shocked at the way I was drawing a line in the sand. Not just a line, but a big deep trench. Seeing Claudia in my wedding dress had made me realise how much I wanted to be a bride. Not just any bride, but Alessandro's bride. How could I settle for anyone else? How could I want anyone else when he was the only one who had ever made me feel alive?

'Then maybe it's best if we don't see each other again,' he said, with a note of finality that slammed into my heart like a wrecking ball.

'How am I going to explain that to Claudia?' I asked. 'How are *you* going to explain it? She thinks we're best friends.'

He let out a long, uneven breath. 'I'll enrol her in a different school.'

'But she's doing so *well*!' I said. 'She's made friends. She's secure—probably for the first time in her little life. How can you uproot her just because you can't face a bit of commitment?'

His jaw locked and he snatched up his keys from where he'd left them on the kitchen bench. 'I have to go. I'll be back in the morning to pick up Claudia. It wouldn't be fair to wake her up now.'

I folded my arms across my chest and jerked my chin towards the door. 'That's right. You go. Walk away when it all gets too difficult. That's what I did. I didn't stay around long enough to hear your explanation of why you hadn't told me about your ex. It takes guts to stick around and hear the truth. It takes guts to step out of your comfort zone. To admit you need and love someone.'

Our gazes collided. Then meshed. My heart contracted. I could already read his mind. Apparently my mother isn't the only one in our family with psychic abilities.

'I wish I could give you what you want but I can't,' he said. 'There's too much at stake. I think it's best if we end our...fling. It will be fairer on you. On me and on Claudia.'

'Fine.'

I said it so matter-of-factly I almost believed it. Almost.

I was even brave enough to follow him to the door and wave him off, as if he was just another tea-party guest who had enjoyed the result of my labours in the kitchen.

It was only when the door had closed that I allowed myself to let a couple of tears squeeze past my eyelids. I blinked to stem the flow, took a deep breath, and brushed my hand across my face.

It was only then that I saw Claudia standing in the doorway, with the bundle of her bedding and a woebegone look on her face.

'I'm sorry,' she said in a whisper-soft voice. 'I had a bad d-d-dream and I wet the bed.'

CHAPTER TWELVE

IT TOOK A WHILE to sort out the bed, Claudia's shower, and an explanation of why her uncle and I were apparently not best friends any more. I sat beside her as I tucked her in and tried my best to explain.

'It's not that we don't love each other. It's... complicated.'

'Is it because you're my teacher?'

'No, nothing like that,' I said, wishing it was that simple.

'Then why c-c-can't you be together?'

Good question.

'Because there are other issues,' I said.

'Is it because of my mummy?'

I looked down at her earnest little face. How much did she know? How much had she guessed?

'Your uncle is doing everything he can to help your mummy get better,' I said.

Claudia's little fingers plucked at the hem of the sheet. 'My mummy might never get better.'

My chest tightened at the worldly pragmatism in her statement. She was six years old. *Six!* How had she become so jaded?

'We should never give up hope,' I said, hugging her close and resting my chin on her little head. 'On anybody.'

Good advice, I thought.

If only I had the courage to believe it.

Once Claudia was asleep I went back to the sitting room. I glanced at my phone. Suddenly I could think of no viable excuse not to call my mother.

I reached for it just as it began to ring.

'Mum?' I said. 'I was just about to call you. I'm sorry for what I said. It was so insensitive of me, given the circumstances, and I—'

'Poppet, I'm the one who's supposed to be apologising,' my mother said. 'I had no idea that horrible thing had happened to you.'

She began to cry, and the rest became a bit garbled as we swapped apologies and sorted out some stuff.

I hadn't realised how terribly controlling my grandparents had been towards my mother. They dictated everything to her. She'd felt like an item on an assembly line. By the age of five her whole life had been mapped out for her. What friends she would play with. What subjects she would study at school and at university. What career she would have. What man she would marry. Where she would live.

She wasn't just a square peg in a round hole. She was a feather that needed to float free. My father had much the same kind of upbringing, which was why he had bonded with my mother. They weren't perfect. But they were my parents and it was about time I accepted them for all their foibles.

We ended the call with a lot of 'I love you's and kissy smoochy noises.

Yes. Even some from me.

* * *

Alessandro arrived the next morning to pick up Claudia. We were so polite to each other it was nauseating. It was back to Dr Lucioni and Miss Clark.

I stood back as he led Claudia to his car, but just before he closed the car door she jumped back out and ran towards me. Her little body cannoned into mine and hugged me so tightly I couldn't breathe. Or maybe that was because my emotions had taken up all the space inside my chest.

'I love you, Jem,' she said.

I bent and hugged her back, and kissed the top of her head. 'I love you too, sweetie. But you have to call me Miss Clark tomorrow, remember?'

She looked up at me with those big brown eyes that so reminded me of her uncle's.

'I want to live with you for ever and ever. I want to be with you instead of at the boarding house. C-c-c-can't I stay with you?'

I glanced at Alessandro's face. His jaw was tight, but I noticed his throat was moving up and down over a swallow. His eyes looked red and pained, as if the sunlight was too bright—even though there wasn't any sunlight. Well, not much to speak of. It was a grey morning, with clouds that hung oppressively overhead in clotted knots of gloom.

I bent down so I was face to face with Claudia. 'Sweetie, I'll see you every day at school. I'm not going anywhere.'

Claudia's bottom lip wobbled. 'But I heard Uncle Alessandro say last night I'm going to a new school. I don't want to go to another school. I want to stay at *your* school.'

Alessandro bent down and put his arm around Claudia's thin little shoulders. His knees were almost touching mine. This close, I could smell the clean sharp citrus of his aftershave. I could also see a tiny nick on his jaw where he'd cut himself shaving.

A top-notch surgeon who's cut himself shaving? I thought. He was definitely having a bad day.

'If you want to stay at Miss Clark's school that's fine, *mio piccolo*,' he said.

I pushed in Claudia's pouting bottom lip with my fingertip. 'No more tears, okay? Everything's going to work out just fine.'

Alessandro met my gaze. 'Jem... Can I see you tonight?'

I was conscious of little ears listening eagerly. 'I think we've said all that needs to be said. No point dragging things on unnecessarily.'

His eyes refused to let mine go. The intensity of his gaze made something in my heart give a little jerk.

'All right,' he said. 'I'll say it now. I love you. I fell in love with you that day in Paris, when you spilled the contents of your handbag at my feet.'

Claudia's little face started to beam and she clasped her hands together like she was mentally saying a prayer.

I moistened my lips and tried to look casually indifferent. *So what?* I wanted to say. *You obviously don't love me enough to marry me.* But instead I retreated into one of my stubborn silences.

'I couldn't believe I'd found someone so funny, so intelligent, so witty—so perfect for me,' he went on. 'I should never have let you go. I'm still not sure why I did. But one thing I do know. I'm not going to do it again. I don't want to lose you a second time. It would be like losing my future, losing any chance of happiness. I can't bear to face the rest of my life without you in it. I want to see you every day. I want you to make me laugh every day, with your twisted sense of humour. I want to make *you* laugh. I want to take away the hurts you've hidden away for all this time. Will you marry me, my darling?'

I was having trouble seeing past the blurry tears in my eyes. Claudia was looking up at me expectantly. Alessandro was looking at me like a man who was wearing his heart on his sleeve. A tricky manoeuvre even for a top-notch heart surgeon, I thought.

'What changed your mind?' I asked.

I'm all for a bit of grovelling. I figured he owed me that much after the hellish nights without sleep I'd been through. Make that five years of hellish nights.

'I went back to my house last night,' he said. 'That great old empty shell of a house I'm spending so much money and time and effort on—but for what? What's the point of me making it into something special when I have no one special to share it with? My *life's* like an empty shell without you in it. I don't want to spend the rest of my life without you. The last five years have been bad enough. I know it's hard to juggle stuff, but other people seem to manage. We'll find a way to manage. *I'll* find a way. Please say yes. Please say you'll marry me.'

My heart was so full of love and joy it was leaving me little room to breathe. I'm pretty sure my face was radiant with happiness. I figured it wouldn't matter if the sun never came out again. I was doing its job for it. Everyone would be blaming *me* for global warming before too long.

'I've always wanted a man to get down on bended knee to propose to me,' I said. 'I didn't realise I'd be on bended knee as well, with half the street watching.'

Alessandro grinned. 'Are the curtains twitching?'

'Numbers four to ten,' I said. 'Number three and seven are out on their front steps.'

His brow suddenly wrinkled in puzzlement. 'How do you know when you've got your back to them?'

Actually, I had no idea how I knew. Freaky!

'A wild guess,' I said.

'Then we'd better not disappoint them,' he said. 'Will you do me the honour of being my wife and the mother of my children?'

'*And* being my aunty!' Claudia piped up.

I laughed and cuddled her close—which brought me even closer to Alessandro, so our mouths were just about touching. 'Yes,' I said. 'Yes, to both of you.'

Alessandro's mouth sealed mine. Claudia's little rosebud lips kissed my cheek and then his. Moistly. Noisily. My mother was going to *love* this little kid, I thought.

My neighbours clapped and cheered.

Our kiss went on for such a long time even Claudia got fed up.

She tapped each of us on the shoulder. 'Aren't you finished *yet*?' she said, eyes rolling.

Alessandro cupped my face in his hands, his dark brown gaze glinting. 'I'm just getting started,' he said.

My phone rang before he could kiss me again. I know. Crap timing. I *knew* it was my mother. Don't ask me how. Maybe I *am* a little psychic.

'Mum,' I said. 'I have something to tell you—'

'I know, poppet,' my mother said. 'You're getting married.'

'How on earth do you know *that*?' I asked, glancing at Alessandro again to see if he was responsible. But he gave a 'beats me' gesture with his upturned hands.

It kind of showed how much he 'got' my parents. They would have been appalled if he'd gone to ask my father for my hand in marriage. How I would get my father to give me away was going to be an exercise in diplomacy or bribery...or something. Then there was the issue of getting my parents inside a church...

Yikes. Fun times ahead.

'I had a vision last night,' my mother said. 'You were wearing this gorgeous white taffeta and tulle dress and you had a little girl with dark hair and big brown eyes as your flower girl.'

I smiled at Claudia and whispered, 'Will you be my flower girl?'

Her little face lit up like a beacon. *'Yes!'*

But there was one person my mother left out of her vision.

Five months later I had *two* bridesmaids, as well as a flower girl—my sister, Bertie, and Alessandro's sister Bianca.

I couldn't have asked for more.

* * * * *

MILLS & BOON®
Hardback – June 2015

ROMANCE

The Bride Fonseca Needs	Abby Green
Sheikh's Forbidden Conquest	Chantelle Shaw
Protecting the Desert Heir	Caitlin Crews
Seduced into the Greek's World	Dani Collins
Tempted by Her Billionaire Boss	Jennifer Hayward
Married for the Prince's Convenience	Maya Blake
The Sicilian's Surprise Wife	Tara Pammi
Russian's Ruthless Demand	Michelle Conder
His Unexpected Baby Bombshell	Soraya Lane
Falling for the Bridesmaid	Sophie Pembroke
A Millionaire for Cinderella	Barbara Wallace
From Paradise...to Pregnant!	Kandy Shepherd
Midwife...to Mum!	Sue MacKay
His Best Friend's Baby	Susan Carlisle
Italian Surgeon to the Stars	Melanie Milburne
Her Greek Doctor's Proposal	Robin Gianna
New York Doc to Blushing Bride	Janice Lynn
Still Married to Her Ex!	Lucy Clark
The Sheikh's Secret Heir	Kristi Gold
Carrying A King's Child	Katherine Garbera

MILLS & BOON®
Large Print – June 2015

ROMANCE

The Redemption of Darius Sterne	Carole Mortimer
The Sultan's Harem Bride	Annie West
Playing by the Greek's Rules	Sarah Morgan
Innocent in His Diamonds	Maya Blake
To Wear His Ring Again	Chantelle Shaw
The Man to Be Reckoned With	Tara Pammi
Claimed by the Sheikh	Rachael Thomas
Her Brooding Italian Boss	Susan Meier
The Heiress's Secret Baby	Jessica Gilmore
A Pregnancy, a Party & a Proposal	Teresa Carpenter
Best Friend to Wife and Mother?	Caroline Anderson

HISTORICAL

The Lost Gentleman	Margaret McPhee
Breaking the Rake's Rules	Bronwyn Scott
Secrets Behind Locked Doors	Laura Martin
Taming His Viking Woman	Michelle Styles
The Knight's Broken Promise	Nicole Locke

MEDICAL

Midwife's Christmas Proposal	Fiona McArthur
Midwife's Mistletoe Baby	Fiona McArthur
A Baby on Her Christmas List	Louisa George
A Family This Christmas	Sue MacKay
Falling for Dr December	Susanne Hampton
Snowbound with the Surgeon	Annie Claydon

MILLS & BOON®
Hardback – July 2015

ROMANCE

MILLS & BOON®
Large Print – July 2015

ROMANCE

The Taming of Xander Sterne	Carole Mortimer
In the Brazilian's Debt	Susan Stephens
At the Count's Bidding	Caitlin Crews
The Sheikh's Sinful Seduction	Dani Collins
The Real Romero	Cathy Williams
His Defiant Desert Queen	Jane Porter
Prince Nadir's Secret Heir	Michelle Conder
The Renegade Billionaire	Rebecca Winters
The Playboy of Rome	Jennifer Faye
Reunited with Her Italian Ex	Lucy Gordon
Her Knight in the Outback	Nikki Logan

HISTORICAL

The Soldier's Dark Secret	Marguerite Kaye
Reunited with the Major	Anne Herries
The Rake to Rescue Her	Julia Justiss
Lord Gawain's Forbidden Mistress	Carol Townend
A Debt Paid in Marriage	Georgie Lee

MEDICAL

How to Find a Man in Five Dates	Tina Beckett
Breaking Her No-Dating Rule	Amalie Berlin
It Happened One Night Shift	Amy Andrews
Tamed by Her Army Doc's Touch	Lucy Ryder
A Child to Bind Them	Lucy Clark
The Baby That Changed Her Life	Louisa Heaton

0615 GEN STD LP

MILLS & BOON®

Why shop at millsandboon.co.uk?

Each year, thousands of romance readers find their perfect read at millsandboon.co.uk. That's because we're passionate about bringing you the very best romantic fiction. Here are some of the advantages of shopping at www.millsandboon.co.uk:

* **Get new books first**—you'll be able to buy your favourite books one month before they hit the shops

* **Get exclusive discounts**—you'll also be able to buy our specially created monthly collections, with up to 50% off the RRP

* **Find your favourite authors**—latest news, interviews and new releases for all your favourite authors and series on our website, plus ideas for what to try next

* **Join in**—once you've bought your favourite books, don't forget to register with us to rate, review and join in the discussions

Visit **www.millsandboon.co.uk**
for all this and more today!